Published by Alan Kilpatrick

Cover design by Alan Kilpatrick
Images from www.shutterstock.com

Book I
The Glass People

Alan Kilpatrick

‘Whoever finds their life will lose it, and whoever loses their life for my sake will find it.’
(Jesus)

For Jan, Jas & Joel, Sunday, Keziah, Nathan and Rowan

A story for children of all ages

Prologue

In a world full of glass the most frightening thing is a red-hot furnace. A furnace so hot that if any glass gets near it, the glass starts to melt. The furnace in the house on the hill was such a furnace. Large. Red-hot and bubbling. With steps into it and steps out of it. The furnace burned continually and the heat was intense. The furnace was in the home of the Glassmaker. He made everything out of glass and was continually tending the furnace. It was a beautiful house with many rooms and many doors. The house sat in the countryside on its own, with no other neighbours. Bird's flew between the eaves of the house and animals dwelt in peace in the gardens surrounding it. The sun shone and all was well. If we were high in the clouds we could zoom out and see what surrounds the garden and house. We would see mountains and rivers and a beautiful waterfall. Looking further away we would see a village - the village of Knock. The place where the heroes of our story live.

Chapter 1 - Knock

The village of Knock lay at the bottom of a large hill. Trees covered the slopes of the hill, but at the top was a clearing where the hill stood higher than the tops of the trees and you could see all around the country. On the other side the village was bordered by a lake, a beautiful, blue lake - in fact it was called 'The Blue Lake' - not a very imaginative name, I know, but it was very blue! The blue lake was a wonderful place to fish. There were so many different types of fish - smackerels, snouts, jumping jacks, belly face groupers (because their mouths looked like belly buttons!) and many, many more. All were tasty and lovely to eat. Day in and out fishermen would go into the lake to fish and return laden with lots of different types, birds following them hoping for a bite of lunch.

The quay, where the fishermen landed their catches, was full of activity - and very smelly, because of the fish. Dogs chased cats and fishwives shouted at their husbands for being out fishing too long. Children ran in between all of the adults, causing people to stumble and fall over into piles of smelly fish. People called out at market stalls trying to encourage others to come and buy their products. They shouted, 'Belly faced Groupers - two for a penny' or 'Three loaves of bread for a thrupence' or 'Apples - penny a bag'. It was very much like a chaotic village scene from a village in our world. Except for one important thing - everything was made of glass!

Chapter 2 - Glass

Now this may seem very strange to us - a world made of glass - isn't glass dangerous? To us it is - so please be careful and don't ever play with real glass. But to the people of the glass world it was completely normal. They had glass sandwiches, ate glass apples and had glass beds. They caught glass fish in glass nets out of glass fishing boats. Everything was made of glass and it was completely normal to them. But if you looked closely at everything you noticed that they all had one thing in common (apart from being made of glass) - everything had cracks and chips. From the blades of grass to the people - everything was scratched and broken. Boats had cracks in the hulls. Men had one ear (the other had fallen off) and they always said 'Pardon!' Some birds had one wing and would fly around in circles. Some fishermen had nets with holes so big that they never caught any fish! This world had been created by the Glassmaker. It had been made perfect, but over time it had become chipped, cracked and broken. Even though they could people never went to the Glassmaker to be repaired because they were too afraid of him and most of them didn't really believe He was real anyway.

Chapter 3 - Three Friends

In this broken village of Knock, inhabited by broken people, lived three children. They were called Daniel, Jonah and Ruth. Daniel was of average height, had dark hair and green eyes. Daniel was the one who was last when they were doing something naughty - not because he was a goody-two shoes but because he was scared. Jonah was the shortest of the three (and the roundest!). His nose kept falling off and he had to stick it to his face with tape. Jonah worried about everything. As we have said, Daniel would be the last one into doing something naughty, but Jonah would be the first to run away after he had done something naughty as he'd be worried about being caught and not getting his pocket money. Ruth was always getting annoyed with the boys because she thought that their tricks and jokes were rubbish and that hers were much better. But the boys never listened to her - and that annoyed her.

As we enter the village the three friends were running as fast as they can. Running to safety and away from the village policeman - Constable Bunce. He was cross! He had just walked into a room at the school and the three children had placed a bucket of cold water on top of the door that Constable Bunce had to go through to get into the room. The ice-cold water had fallen on top of him! The three children laughed and then they saw the angry stare of Constable Bunce and so they ran. The Constable, who was rather large and unfit, was trying to catch them, but he couldn't and instead was huffing and wheezing. The children ran further away, laughing and as they rounded a corner Daniel hit the edge of the wall with his shoulder and chipped it.

'Oww!' he cried, as they continued running not able to pick up the small piece that had broken off.

'Oh my goodness we will get into such trouble' said Jonah.

'Keep running' cried Daniel, 'He still might be able to catch us.'

'Don't be such a scaredy cat, Daniel. There is no way that Constable Bunce can catch us now. It was a stupid idea anyway', said Ruth.

'No it wasn't', said Jonah (whose idea it was).

'Yes it was', cried Daniel and Ruth together, at which point they all burst out laughing again and slowed down and hid in an alleyway, until they were sure that Constable Bunce had stopped his pursuit.

Daniel examined his shoulder, which was cracked and painful. There was no hiding now that they had been up to mischief.

It was tea-time and the three had to go to their own homes - which they were not happy about as they were sure that their parents would have heard about their trick and be ready to tell them off.

Chapter 4 - The Glassmaker's House

All of the houses were made of glass and they were very similar to an igloo. Thick blocks of cracked glass placed on top of each other until they met at the top. A hole was left in the roof to let smoke escape. Daniel walked to his family home, nervous of the welcome he would receive.

'Why do we do these things?', he thought to himself, regretting what they had done. 'But it was funny', he smiled to himself, holding his cracked shoulder.

He walked through the door of his home. The fire was burning in the middle and his family - mother Martha, father Peter and sister Sarah - were all standing waiting for him with Constable Bunce.

'Oh' said Daniel.

'Oh, indeed', replied his father.

'I'll be off now', said Constable Bunce, who put on his helmet, walked to the door, looked sternly at Daniel and walked out.

Daniel kicked the floor and pursed his lips as his family looked at him in silence.

His father walked over to him.

'Have you anything to say for yourself?'

Daniel said nothing.

'What am I going to do with you?' his father's voice

getting louder, ' you are on triple chores for the rest of your life! I will send you to the Glassmakers furnace if you keep doing this!'

At this point Daniel's mother saw his chipped shoulder and came quickly to his side.

She bent down beside him and started to fuss over his shoulder.

'Serves him right if he hurt himself', said his sister Sarah, who gave him a 'you're-in-trouble' smile.

'Leave him alone, Martha', said his father.

'Peter, he has hurt himself and it needs tending. He will do extra chores for a long time. Don't get so angry with him.'

Peter sighed, knowing his wife was right, and went to sit down beside the fire as Martha sorted Daniel's shoulder as best she could.

'I'm sorry Daniel for saying that I would send you to the Glassmaker's furnace. I was angry', said Peter as his children sat at his feet by the fire.

'Is there really a furnace, Daddy?', asked Sarah.

'People say there is. A huge, red-hot furnace that is ready to melt any glass'.

The children looked scared, eyes wide open and Daniel hid behind the seat.

Their father suddenly jumped out of his seat and made a roaring sound. The children fell back on the floor in fear and then realised that their father was joking. Peter threw himself on the floor beside his children and started to tickle them and through the tickles Daniel thought, 'I truly love my family'.

'Is it real, though?', asked Daniel.

'No, it's just a myth'.

'But what about the house that we can see far away on the hill', said Daniel, 'Is that not the Glassmaker's house and isn't the furnace in there?'

In a world made of glass the scariest thing is a red hot

furnace.

'Some people say that the house on the hill is the Glassmaker's house and that there is a furnace in it, but nobody knows for sure. If there is a Glassmaker, then why doesn't He come and help us?'

'Don't talk like that in front of the children', replied his wife.

'Why not?', said Peter, 'its true - if He made us and cares for us then why is He not here helping us?'

'We could go to him', said Daniel.

As he said this everyone looked at him as though he had just said the silliest thing ever.

Chapter 5 - Attack

The next day, after Daniel had finished triple chores, the three friends climbed through the forest on the hill to their favourite spot - the clearing at the top of the hill where they could see everything. As they climbed through the forest glass, squirrels scurried away and ran up the trees and birds flew through the leaves, singing at the top of their voices. Daniel, Jonah and Ruth played hide and seek behind the tree trunks as they climbed closer to the clearing and talked about the upcoming thanksgiving celebration - the day when all families gathered together in the streets and celebrated summer.

'I cannot wait for Mrs Ferwinckle's cakes. They are the best', said Jonah.

'You are always thinking of your stomach', joked Daniel.

'No I am not. I just appreciate good baking!'

'Your large stomach shows your appreciation' said Ruth as she ran away from Jonah, who was now chasing her.

They eventually reached the top of the hill and entered into the clearing, where they all stood in silence looking into the distance. Daniel looked at the pin-prick of a house that people said was the Glassmakers home and wondered what the truth about the Glassmaker was.

'Oh, I cannot wait for the boar on the spit - that's always

the best part', Jonah was still talking about the food and the thanksgiving celebration. 'Do you remember last year', he continued, ' when the chair of grumpy Mr Crudge broke and he fell backwards into the bucket of chicken intestines?'

Daniel's attention was taken from the Glassmaker's house by Jonah's comment and they all sat on top of the clearing, laughing.

Sitting in silence and admiring the view, Daniel said, 'I love it here! Despite all the cracks and chips'.

The sun slowly rose, the colour changing from a deep red to yellow. They enjoyed its warmth and they lay back on the glass grass and were thankful.

After a few moments they all heard a strange sound. It sounded like the sound of someone shouting. The noise got louder, and Daniel, Jonah and Ruth all stood up and looked down at the village. Horrified, they saw that smoke was rising from the houses in Knock and that grey, glass men were riding around the village on horse back. The village was under attack.

Chapter 6 - Prisoners

The children couldn't believe what they were seeing. The village had never been attacked before.

'No!', cried Daniel, as he started to run down to help, but stopped as he saw how many soldiers there were.

Jonah stared silently in disbelief, his mouth hanging open.

'We must do something - quickly', urged Ruth

'But, what? There are so many of the grey soldiers - on horses! There is no way we can help, no matter how badly we want to', replied Daniel, a tear running down his cheek.

'You're a coward!', accused Ruth.

Daniel didn't say anything - he just sighed and hung his head.

Jonah was still staring silently.

As he watched, grey soldiers on horseback and on foot went through the village laughing and smashing houses and sinking boats. People were running in every direction trying to escape. Constable Bunce was attempting to bring order but it was hopeless, and he was knocked to the ground by a passing rider.

'Who are these people?', Jonah asked, breaking his silence, tears running down his face.

Ruth had started to run down the hill towards the village.

'I don't know, but I am going to smash them to pieces!

Come on, let's go.'

She ran a little way down the hill before she realised that she was alone. She had expected the boys to follow. She was wrong. They stayed where they were, looking at their precious village and then at Ruth, ashamed because they were too scared.

'Boys are supposed to be brave!' shouted Ruth, furious that the boys hadn't followed her.

The noise of smashing glass stopped and Daniel, Ruth and Jonah watched in despair as they saw everyone in the village rounded up, tied up and lifted on to carts. Their whole village was being taken prisoner.

Chapter 7 - Making a plan

Daniel shouted in anger, fear, loss and many other emotions, but his cry was unheard. He watched helplessly as he saw his family tied up and hauled onto a cart.

He sank to his knees, snot flowing freely. He could see his sister crying, his mother, whose face was full of fear, trying to comfort her.

The families of Ruth and Jonah were taken hostage too.

"We must go and help',said Ruth, tears running down her face, 'we have to rescue them. We are their only hope. We have to, we have to, we have to…'

'But there are too many of them, we would just get captured', said Jonah, ' and then how could we help them?'

'You're just scared', said Ruth.

'Yes I am scared', replied Jonah, 'But what I said is still true!'

In the clearing on top of the hill everything went quiet except for the occasional crash of glass as another house fell down. The village was empty. All their family and friends had been taken prisoner.

Suddenly Daniel noticed that some of the grey soldiers on horses were looking around them, as though they were looking for someone who they had missed. To the children's horror they started to ride through the forest, up the hill towards where they were.

'Run!' Ruth cried out.

At once all three of them started to run away from the village.

One of the difficulties with glass is that when it catches the light is can be like a lighthouse and tell everyone else where you are. That is exactly what happened. The riders saw the glint from the sun shining on the three children's glass bodies and they started to pursue them.

Unaware that they had been seen the children continued to run and run, bumping into rocks and hitting tree branches in their escape, and making more scratches and chips on their little glass bodies.

Daniel suddenly saw a cave in the side of the hill.

'Quick, over here. We can hide in this cave.'

The cave was dark and cold. Water dripped somewhere in the darkness.

The soldiers rode past the children's hiding place and the children breathed a sigh of relief that they were safe - for now.

They continued to stay quiet until they were sure that it was completely safe and that the riders would not come back.

Ruth looked at Daniel who seemed to be deep in thought.

'What are you thinking about?'

'Nothing.'

'Yes you are - you have that look on your face that you have when you are trying to figure something out'

'I am not thinking about anything.'

'Daniel!', shouted Ruth and Jonah together.

After a moment Daniel lifted his eyes and looked at his two friends 'You're not going to like it! The only person that can help us is the Glassmaker. We have to go to his house!'

Chapter 8 - Starting the Journey of a Lifetime

'What!' said Ruth, 'Are you mad!'

'I can't believe you would even think that!' said Jonah ' What on earth are you thinking? We have to be realistic and try and work out some way to get our families back.'

'I am', replied Daniel. 'There's no way that we can do this by ourselves. We need help.'

At this Ruth grabbed Daniel and shook him.

'The Glassmaker is just a myth and even if He is real, why would He want to help us?'

Daniel pushed her away and stood breathing heavily.

'I am not sure about the Glassmaker, whether He is real or not or if He would even help us if we asked him, but for the sake of our families we have to try. There is no other way. I am terrified at the thought of going to the house on the hill, but the thought of my family suffering gives me a little bit of courage. I would do anything for my father and mother, and my sister.

'Wouldn't we all', said Jonah 'but your idea is insane!'

'Maybe, so what do you think we should do?'

Jonah had no idea of what to do and he stayed silent.

'If you don't want to come then fine, but I am going to try and get help.'

At this Daniel stood up and walked out of the cave into the

sunlight, checking to make sure that there were no soldiers lurking about.

Ruth and Jonah stood looking at each other.

'Better than doing nothing', Ruth said and followed Daniel out of the cave leaving Jonah alone.

'Wait for me!', Jonah cried, running after the other two.

Chapter 9 - Grey Soldiers

The sun was shining as the three friends walked gloomily along the barren road. They had gone back to the village after they had left the cave to gather supplies for their journey. The sight of what had once been their homes, smashed and broken, had filled them with sadness and dread and the sense that they just had to take this journey to the Glassmakers house, even if none of them really wanted to. They had to try and rescue their families.

By the time they had reached the farthest point any of them had been before, they had been walking all day and were tired. Actually, no-one they knew had been this far because the people of Knock weren't great travellers. They all stopped and looked at each other. They held hands and took a step forward together. It wasn't long before the heat of the day and the length of the journey tired the children out.

'How far do you think we have to go before we reach the house?' said Jonah, too afraid to use the word Glassmaker.

'I really haven't the foggiest idea', said Ruth sarcastically, 'I've never been there before.'

'Just asking', replied Jonah and he slowed down and walked behind the other two.

'No need to be mean.', said Daniel, 'He's just saying what we are all thinking.'

'Well, I don't know and I don't want to know how long before we get there, as I'm not sure I really want to go there anyway', said Ruth who then strode on ahead also so they all walked separately.

They walked in this way for about half an hour until Jonah ran past them as fast as he could, shouting, 'Run! They're coming!'

Not quite sure who 'they' were, Daniel and Ruth stood still for a moment and turned around to see why Jonah was running. They very quickly started to run as well as they caught sight of four grey soldiers on horses riding quickly towards them.

Chapter 10 - A Forest Hideaway

They weren't sure if the soldiers had seen them or not, so they ran as fast as they possibly could. Hope grew as they saw that they were running towards a forest. They all made for a path in the forest that they could see, and as soon as they were in the forest they left the path and hid in the roots of some enormous trees a short way from the path.

Desperate for air after running they hardly dared breathe, fearful that they would be heard by the passing soldiers. Eventually they heard the hooves of the horses as the riders moved into the forest and started down the path - which was difficult as the path was narrow and branches were at the same height as the riders' faces. After what seemed like an eternity Daniel, Ruth and Jonah could no longer hear the soldiers. The soldiers had left.

Darkness had started to fall and no one talked. Soon all three were fast asleep.

In the darkest part of the night an owl flew near the children. Daniel was awoken by the owl, but then he also heard the crunching of glass underfoot. His heart started to pound as he became fearful that the soldiers had turned back and were moving towards them. He sat up and looked around. All was silent again and he thought he must have dreamt it. He started to lay back down again when out of the corner of his eye he became aware of a growing light. It seemed to be far away, but as he looked he could see that it was getting brighter and closer.

Without saying a word he shook the other two. Annoyed that they had been disturbed, they complained.

'Leave me alone', said Jonah who then turned over and tried to go back to sleep.

Daniel shook him again, 'Wake up!'

Ruth groggily sat up and looked at Daniel. He continued to stare at the light and so Ruth turned around to follow his gaze. She tensed as she saw the light, and she moved closer to Daniel.

Jonah groaned, 'Oh my goodness me, what is the problem - I am so tired and I…' but he never finished his sentence as he saw the light, which was getting closer, lighting up all the surrounding forest, and making the shadows of trees and roots move and flicker as it moved towards them. There was no way of getting away from this light, even if they wanted to. The children were surrounded by the light.

Chapter 11 - A Midnight Encounter

The children shielded their eyes because the light was so bright. It was so bright in contrast to the darkness.

The light stopped moving and started to fade in intensity. As their eyes started to adjust to the light they began to see the outline of a figure. Amazed, and slightly terrified, they saw a beautiful person emerge out of the light. This person had no cracks, no scratches, he was perfect.

'Hello', said the figure, breaking the silence of the night.

The children just stared, not knowing what to do or how to respond.

'Hello', the figure said again, 'My name is Nathaniel. What are yours?'

Daniel, Ruth and Jonah looked at each other and Ruth was the first to speak.

'I'm Ruth.'

'Pleased to meet you.'

'I'm Daniel.'

'I'm Jonah and I'm a wee bit scared of you!'

'No need to be frightened', replied Nathaniel, 'I'm not here to harm you, but to help you'.

'What are you?' asked Daniel.

'I'm like you.'

Jonah laughed. 'You are nothing like us. You are beautiful!'

Nathaniel smiled. 'I am just like you. In fact, I am one of you. I was once scared, alone, cracked and chipped - but not anymore.'

'How is that possible?' said Ruth, doubting what Nathaniel had said.

'I met the Glassmaker and He changed everything. I know why you are running and I know where you want to go. Keep going and don't give up. There will be obstacles but you can overcome them. Stay on the right path. He is waiting for you. Remember His words:

When hands are grabbing for what they can get
Make sure you hold onto that which is best
You can climb the mountain when you see
That letting go will set you free
When stuck in the middle of that which is clear
Push on through and do not fear.'

By this time Nathaniel had started to fade away.

'Wait! Please stay! Is the Glassmaker real? What will happen when we get to the Glassmaker?'

But it was too late - the children were once again plunged into darkness.

Not sure what to say, they said nothing.

Chapter 12 - Doubts And Questions

The three had been confused by what had happened during the night and had eventually drifted off into an uneasy sleep, but all had awoken as soon as the sun started to rise.

"Did that really happen last night or was it a dream?' asked Daniel.

'If it was a dream then it was the most realistic dream I have ever had', stated Jonah, who had been disturbed by the night events the most.

'Whether it was real or not, what did he mean that there would be obstacles? If the Glassmaker wants to see us then why should it be difficult to see him - surely He would make it easy?' said Daniel.

Ruth had been quiet up till now sorting out some breakfast. 'Maybe He wants to see how much we really want to see him', she said.

'Why should He do that?' said Daniel, getting a little bit cross with the whole situation and a big bit frightened, 'I'm not even sure that I want to go to him if He is going to make it difficult to get to him - how silly!'

Jonah was looking at Ruth and then at Daniel as they both started to get frustrated with each other.

'Well, just go home then if you feel frightened', said Ruth, 'I am going to continue as I want to rescue my family even if you don't.'

Well this was the last straw and Daniel shouted at Ruth, 'How dare you say that! I want to rescue my family as much as you do'.

'Well prove it', Ruth replied, and she picked all of her stuff up and walked away from the other two.

Jonah looked at Daniel, picked his things up and then followed Ruth saying, "I'm going with her - she's scary!'

Daniel stood still, staring at the ground as his anger slowly went away. He was frustrated because he knew that Ruth was right - they did have to go on if they wanted to rescue their families. But he was scared.

'Come on Daniel', he said to himself, 'Just take the next step.'

With that he slowly followed the other two.

Chapter 13 - Hands in the River

They had been walking for several hours through a rocky, glass terrain that had made their journey a bit more difficult, when a little stream started to appear. They continued on in silence and slowly the stream started to grow bigger and bigger. The stream soon grew and became very big and very loud as the water rushed quickly past them.

They looked up and down the river realising that the river blocked their progress down the path they were following. They began to get worried as they could see no bridge or boat or any way to cross it.

'How are we going to get across? There's no way', said Jonah

'There must be a way', replied Ruth, but in her heart she was not so sure.

'We just have to go through it', said Daniel, surprising the other two with his brave words.

Daniel stepped gingerly in the edge of the water. The current was very strong, even at the edge. He took a few more steps and although the current was strong it only came up to his waist - even when he had made it into the middle.

'It's not deep, come on!' he cried to his companions.

Ruth and Jonah followed him and they were soon in the middle of the river with him.

Jonah said, 'This is going to be easy'.
But he said it all too soon.
They started to feel something grabbing their legs.

Chapter 14 - Holding Onto Each Other

Panic started to set in as they all tried to rush quickly to the other side of the river, but it soon became impossible.

They looked at the water in horror as they saw hands emerge from the water trying to pull them under. The whole river soon transformed into a mass of hands.

As much as they struggled, they could not get free. They desperately looked at one another and then at the shore.

'Help me!', shouted Jonah as he was pulled further down.

Daniel tried to get closer to him, but he too was pulled further down.

Then Ruth remembered the first two lines of the verse that Nathaniel had told them:

When hands are grabbing for what they can get
Make sure you hold onto that which is best

'We need to hold onto one another - we need each other', she shouted above the roar of the river.

Not quite understanding what she meant, but with no other idea, Daniel and Jonah stretched out and the three were just able to hold each other's hands.

As soon as they did that the horrible hands coming out of the water started to let go as though they had no grip.

Realising that escape was possible, they all moved quickly to the riverbank. It was still difficult, but as they got closer to the edge, the river spat them out onto the ground as though it was fed up with trying to hold onto them.

They were safe.

Chapter 15 - Escape

They tumbled over the rough ground, chipped and scratched a little bit more, but happy to be safe.

They looked back at the river but it was just a normal river now with flowing water. No sign of the hands.

Daniel started to laugh. He was not sure why, but he laughed louder and louder. Ruth and Jonah soon joined in and the three rolled on the ground, relieved that they were alive.

Suddenly Nathaniel appeared. Their laughter stopped and they all looked at him.

Ruth was the first to speak.

'What on earth were those hands? It was terrifying!'

Nathaniel replied, 'They were the hands of people who tried to cross the river without thinking of others. Life is about one another - helping, loving, serving. The only way you crossed the river was by holding each other's hands and helping one another. This meant that the hands in the river had no grip on you. Keep going'

And with that he disappeared.

Jonah said, 'I'm getting a bit fed up with him disappearing before we can ask him any more questions.'

At that Daniel and Ruth burst out laughing again.

Chapter 16 - A Dark Gorge

More chipped and broken than they had ever been before they continued to walk the path for another three days. The surroundings changed as they continued and soon they saw mountains in the distance - small at the moment, but getting bigger with every step they took.

Snow covered the top of the mountains and very soon they were towering over the three travellers.

'There is no way to get over these mountains', said Daniel as he bent backwards to try and see the top of the sheer walls of rock.

They walked along the base of the mountains, their desperation increasing.

'Over here,' shouted Jonah, who had found a dark gorge in the rockface.

When Daniel and Ruth arrived they saw that to enter the gorge they needed to be full of courage as it was very dark and narrow. They didn't have much of that at the moment, but their river crossing had given them a little bit of bravery.

They all knew that they had to continue, but were afraid to take the first step.

Eventually Daniel put out his hands for Ruth and Jonah to hold.

'Come on. If we learnt anything from the river it was that

we have to do this together.'

Ruth and Jonah took his hands and they walked into the deep, dark gorge.

Chapter 17 - Speaking Birds

They were caught by surprise. They had expected to walk through the gorge in darkness, fumbling and feeling their way through. It had been like that for a short distance, but then in the darkness, they had felt cold flakes of something fall on their faces. Frightened that it was something terrible they started to run away in a panic. Then the darkness seemed to fade and they found themselves in a snow scene! Thick snowdrifts banked the sides of the gorge and the snow fell constantly. It was beautiful!

Jonah made a snowball and threw it at Daniel. It hit him on the back of the head, and after the initial shock he too made a snowball and threw it back, hitting Jonah. Soon a full scale snowball fight was in progress, with the children running around, hiding behind rocks and whooping as they hit someone. They all ran at each other with snowballs flying and they slipped on some ice and collapsed in a heap laughing.

'We must get going', said Daniel, 'but only after we have made a snowman.'

They trudged through the snow, happy and cold, when they encountered two paths. Which way should they go? Stay on the right path, Nathaniel had said, but which one was the right path?

'This is unfortunate!' said Ruth, whose teeth had started to chatter.

'It would be really good to have a map!', Jonah said

Three little red-breasted robins were flying around and they stopped on a leafless tree beside the beginning of the paths.

They looked at the children and seemed to be trying to speak to them.

'Are those robins trying to speak to us?' Ruth asked, really not believing that they were.

'Don't be silly - birds don't speak, they chirp or tweet', replied Daniel

'But they really do look like they are trying to speak to us', insisted Ruth

The birds suddenly took flight and flew in circles around the beginning of one of the paths.

'Do you think they are trying to show us the way?', said Daniel

'Or the wrong way!' said Jonah

'I don't think so', said Daniel who had started to follow the path the birds had pointed out.

Jonah followed, grumbling, 'Since when do birds speak and show us the way!'

Chapter 18 - A Wall of Ice

When it became clear to the robins that the children had followed them on to the right path, they flew away. For they were good robins and, as you shall see, the closer you got to the Glassmaker the more magical things became.

'Thank you little birds', shouted Daniel

'Lucky guess', said Jonah, still not sure they were actually on the right path, 'robins are rascals'.

'No, you're the rascal - robins are sweet.'

'No, I am sweet and the robins are rascals!'

Ruth was about to reply when Daniel said, 'Stop bickering. Look the snow is getting deeper'.

And it was true. The snow was falling more heavily and it was definitely getting deeper. It made it so much harder to walk, especially since they had backpacks, filled with food and clothes and tools.

'This is hard work!', said Ruth

'Yes - especially since you filled your backpack with clothes and dresses!' replied Jonah.

Ruth just glared at him.

They trudged on through the thick snow.

'I wish I was a robin - at least I could fly over this snow', said Jonah.

The snow was so heavy now they could barely see in front

of them. Suddenly they all banged into a wall, a wall of ice.

'Ouch', said Jonah, who was picking up his nose, which had fallen off again.

The wall was immense and high. Through the falling snow they could just about see the top, with the three robins perched on it.

'Show offs!', yelled Jonah

On the wall of ice there were bits of ice jutting out.

'I wonder if we could climb up using those bits of ice as foot holds', wondered Daniel

'Those aren't bits of ice', said Ruth, whose voice was shaky, 'They are people!'

Chapter 19 - Leaving Everything

The children were horrified as they looked up the sheer face of the wall of ice. They staggered backwards and fell onto the cold ground.

As they were looking up they saw a figure at the top alongside the robins - it was Nathaniel!

He floated down from the top of the wall and was soon standing beside the children.

Still shaken by the sight of the frozen people stuck to the wall they stood up and looked at Nathaniel.

He smiled at them.

'You're wondering who these unfortunate people are'.

They all nodded.

'Like the people who were captured by the river, these are people who were on the same journey as you, but they have been stuck to the wall'.

Ruth was looking at the frozen people.

'Why didn't they make it? Why didn't they get to the top? Why did they get stuck?'

Ruth had so many questions.

'The people tried to climb this wall with everything they had brought with them. They attempted to climb with their backpacks, pots, pans, clothes, food, money, but all of that was too heavy and they took too long to climb, and so they were frozen to the wall'.

The children were visibly shaken by what he said.

Nathaniel continued, 'If you want to get over this wall then you have to leave everything behind. Everything'.

This was a frightening thought. Leave everything. How would they survive? What would they eat?

Knowing their thoughts Nathaniel said, 'Don't worry about anything. Do you not remember what I said to you:

You can climb the mountain when you see
That letting go will set you free'.

The children looked at each other.

Daniel was the first to speak, 'We have no choice. We've come this far, we can't turn back', and with that he threw all his belongings to the ground.

The strangest thing happened. Daniel started to float. He got higher and higher and was nearly at the top of the wall when the other two quickly threw off their belongings and they too started to float!

Chapter 20 - A Horrible Discovery

They floated past all of the people who had tried to hold onto to their belongings, but had got stuck on the wall. It was a horrible sight. They were all so glad to reach the top of the wall and even more so when they had stopped floating and landed on the ground.

They smiled at one another and couldn't quite believe what had just happened.

The robins were still at the top of the wall and were flying around them. One of them landed on Jonah's shoulder and promptly started to talk!

'Welcome, welcome, welcome!' it said, 'We are so glad you made it. It has been such a long time since anyone has'.

Jonah was so surprised that he fell to the ground again.

The birds chirped all the more at that and Jonah thought they were laughing at him. Nathaniel had floated up the wall as well and was laughing at Jonah, but he didn't stop at the top he kept on floating until he disappeared from sight.

'I've never heard an animal talk before', said Daniel.

'None of us have. It's amazing!', said Jonah.

One of the robins landed on Ruth's head.

'The closer you get to the Glassmaker the more magical it becomes.', the bird tweeted.

'Will there be more amazing things?', asked Ruth.

'So much more', the bird replied, 'But for now you must keep going. Slide down this slope and it will lead you to the path you must follow.'

The children thanked the birds for helping them and as they flew off, the three friends slid down the icy slope - it was scary and exciting at the same time. They could see the end of the gorge as it was getting lighter and lighter and soon they were thrown out of the dark gorge into bright sunshine.

Chapter 21 - Monster In The Sky

The children lay enjoying the warmth of the sun after the coldness of the dark gorge.

The grass was soft and birds and insects flew around their heads. It was wonderful to relax after their last adventure.

When they had left all of their backpacks behind at the foot of the ice wall they had been worried about what they would eat as all of their food had been in the bags. But now they saw that they need not have worried at all. There were fruit trees growing in this land. Fruits with amazing flowers, and of different varieties and size. They ran around the trees picking up different types of fruit and eating them, encouraging each other to try the fruit they had just eaten. It was so sweet, so juicy, so filling.

It wasn't long before the children needed another nap because they had eaten so much.

They were lying in the grass in the warm sun when suddenly Daniel sat up abruptly.

'Did you see that?', he said with a trembling voice, pointing to the sky above.

'See what?', said Ruth, straining her eyes to try and see what Daniel had seen.

After a moment she also saw it - a huge, winged monster flying through the air, moving quickly this way and that way as though it was being chased. But who on earth or what would that monster be frightened off?

'Quickly - hide!'

They quickly moved to find cover in case the monster saw them and attacked them. Hearts racing they followed the movements of the creature from their hiding place and then, suddenly, the monster stopped flying and started to fall as though it had been injured. It then disappeared from sight altogether.

Daniel, Ruth and Jonah didn't wait to discuss what they had just seen - they started to run towards the Glassmaker's house!

Chapter 22 - A Magical Waterfall

Completely confused by what they had just seen, the children ran towards a forest that they had spotted in the distance.

'Let's hide in the forest', cried Daniel.

They stopped on the edge of the forest, unsure whether they should go in, as the place they thought would give them safety now looked very scary close-up.

'I'm not going in there', said Jonah backing away from the enormous trees.

'Where are you going to go? You can't go back - there's nothing there and you don't know what else is going on in the sky that we can't see', replied Ruth staring at the forest.

Jonah looked up into the sky and recalled the enormous flying monster that they had seen. He sighed, knowing that Ruth was right. They had to go into the forest. They had to get to the Glassmaker.

'What's going to happen to us in here?' asked Jonah walking into the forest.

It was hard work. The trees were gigantic with huge roots coming out of the ground that were covered with a deep green slippery moss. The children had to scramble over the slippery roots and were constantly hurting their knees and shins.

Even so, the children's determination to get through the

forest and into the Glassmaker's house was growing. They were becoming more and more confident and their fear was getting less and less. They had overcome two obstacles - together and with some help. Whatever they now faced they all started to believe that they could finish the journey. At this point they had forgotten about the roaring furnace!

The noise of animals and birds was getting quieter, but another noise was growing. As they continued through the forest it got louder.

Soon they came upon the source of the noise. An enormous waterfall, crashing down onto the rocks below. On either side were trees. They were so big you couldn't see the top of them. There was no way round the wall of trees and no way to climb them as the bottom of the trees had no branches to climb up.

However, through the waterfall they could see another land, a garden that was always changing in the flow of the water. They could see the blurred outline of the Glassmaker's house and they realised that they were nearly at their goal. The only way that they could see to get there was to go through the waterfall!

Chapter 23 - Entering The Waterfall

Suddenly they heard shouts from the forest. The enemy soldiers had not stopped looking and somehow had discovered the children. They were in danger.

With the memory of the flying monster still fresh, and the shouts of the enemy soldiers nearby, they all ran towards the waterfall, knowing this was their only option.

Daniel picked up a stone and threw it into the cascading water. The stone entered the water and then simply hung in the water, moving down very slowly to the ground. Ruth picked up another stone and threw it into the water and it did the same. This time the stone was spat out of the water and hit Jonah on the nose, who yelled in pain.

'Sorry Jonah', said Ruth, eyes still fixed on the water.

Daniel said, 'What shall we do?'

Jonah said nothing. He stepped forward and walked into the waterfall.

Chapter 24 - Pushing Through

Time stood still for Jonah - or that's what it felt like to him. He could hardly move. It was like being stuck in a jar of treacle (not that I have ever been stuck in a jar of treacle!). He could see the others outside and then he saw the soldiers emerge from the trees - they were all moving so fast compared to him. He started to panic and tried to wriggle through. He could move, but ever so slowly. Not only was it difficult to move but the water was pressing him into the ground and he was finding it difficult to breathe. He pushed on.

By this time the other two had entered the water and they too were moving slowly through towards Jonah. They were having real difficulty breathing and their hearts were pounding as their bodies cried out for air.

They were close enough to each other to hold hands when they heard the splash of the soldiers as they entered the waterfall. They were so close to the three children, but they were also having trouble moving and breathing.

Jonah was nearly out of breath now but he was nearly at the other side of the waterfall. He was almost fainting. He closed his eyes and thought of his family, tied up and taken hostage by an unknown enemy. He remembered what Nathaniel had said,

'When stuck in the middle of that which is clear
Push on through and do not fear'

The picture of those he loved suffering, and the encouragement of Nathaniel, gave him the extra bit of strength that he needed and he pushed one last time, knowing that it would be his last push if he didn't get clear from the water.

Jonah suddenly disappeared. Ruth and Daniel soon followed him, all three landing flat out on beautiful long green grass. They all quickly got to their knees to see if the soldiers were coming. After a few minutes they relaxed. The soldiers must have turned back. They sat down and looked around and were confronted with the most beautiful garden they had ever seen.

Chapter 25 - The Glassmaker's Garden

It took their breath away. There were colours of the richest blues, greens and reds, the deepest purples and brightest yellows. It almost blinded them. Then there was the fruit. Fruit they recognised and fruit they had never seen before. Huge apples. Enormous oranges. Massive grapes. Not to mention the flowers. Daisies taller than the children, in multiple colours, swaying in the breeze. The strange thing was that they seemed to follow the children, looking at them and smiling. Scented roses with no thorns filled the air with heady fragrances.

Daniel cried out, 'Duck, quickly', as a massive winged insect flew by. The children were convinced that it said 'Good morning' to them.

'Did you hear that?', said Ruth

Puzzled, Daniel was scratching his head, 'No it couldn't be. Insects don't talk'.

'Excuse us', came a voice from the ground. They looked down and saw a line of ants that were being blocked from going forward by Jonah's foot.

'Oh, sorry', said Jonah, who then said, 'Argh, did I just apologise to ants?'

They looked at one another, unsure at what this all meant. They remembered the saying, 'The closer you get to the

Glassmaker the more magical things become', but talking ants!

'Have you noticed something else?' said Ruth.

'What?' said Daniel watching as the line of ants disappeared into the distance.

'Nothing in this garden is scratched or broken or chipped. Everything is perfect'.

'No, it can't be', said Jonah but as he spoke the words his eyes told him that it was true. Everything in the garden was perfect.

Chapter 26 - Deep Sleep

As the children realised that everything in the garden was good and perfect, they had become more aware of how broken and dirty they were themselves. They hadn't realised just how scratched they had become until they stood beside the perfect flowers and fruit. It made them sad, but they also realised that the only one that could help was the Glassmaker, and so they continued on towards the house which was closer than ever - they would reach it very soon.

Daniel was picking some fruit off a tree when something caught his eye around the other side of the tree trunk. It was a foot in the grass. No - it was a whole person. Several people. Terrified, he stumbled backwards and cried out.

'Quick, over here.'

Ruth and Jonah came running to see what was wrong. Daniel just stood there pointing at the bodies lying on the ground.

'Are they d..d.dead?' said Jonah, eyes wide open.

'I'm not sure', said Daniel, his voice trembling

'Hello', called Ruth.

'Shh', shouted the other two

Ruth ignored them. 'Hello' she called again.

There was no answer. Ruth took a step towards the bodies.

'Ruth, don't..', said Jonah, running to hide behind a tree

trunk.

Ruth continued. She reached the group of bodies on the ground and quietly knelt down beside one.

'They're only sleeping', and she shook one to try and wake them. But there was no response. She tried another person. Again, no response.

'What's wrong with them?' asked Daniel who had worked up the courage to come closer.

'I don't know. They are in the deepest sleep that I have seen anyone in.'

'I must confess that I am getting a bit tired', said Jonah, wandering nervously up behind the other two.

A noise in the distance distracted them from the sleeping people.

'Soldiers', shouted Daniel, 'Run!'.

Chapter 27 - Animals Appear

Panic set in as they saw that the soldiers had come through the waterfall. Initially the children ran in different directions as the soldiers chased them, but eventually they all ended up running in the same direction, bumping into tree trunks, tripping over sleeping people and slipping in the grass.

Even though they had not run very far they soon began to feel very drowsy. Their vision started to blur and they couldn't focus on where they were going.

'What's happening to us?' cried Daniel.

'I don't know', said Jonah in a sleepy kind of way, his speech slurring as he was getting too tired to speak.

Ruth could see the soldiers gaining ground. 'Keep going! They are going to catch us if we stop'. But she too was finding it difficult to keep running.

'It feels like someone has attached weights to my legs. I can hardly move', said Daniel, falling to his knees yawning, 'I'm so tired'.

'Don't..', yelled Ruth but she was of no help as she was sitting on the ground lying against a tree trunk and rubbing her eyes, 'Got to keep...'.

But it was too late. All three of them were in the deepest of sleeps as more soldiers burst through the waterfall.

This was when the animals came to help.

Chapter 28 - Helpful Animals

Three horses appeared, one beside each of the children and knelt down beside them. Other animals gathered around them as though in a protective circle.

'Wake up!', yelled a monkey, as he shook the children.

'Try again', suggested a nearby pig, 'You didn't shake them hard enough'.

'Alright, alright', said the monkey, who was called Albert, and he shook them again.

Slowly the children started to wake up, but they thought they were still dreaming when they saw that a monkey was waking them up.

'You're in my dream', said Jonah to the other two and then looking at the monkey said, 'Hello nice baboon!'.

The monkey was very cross.

'No, you're in my dream' said Daniel, 'and it's not a baboon but an orang-utang'.

By this time the monkey was furious and all the other animals were shaking with laughter.

'Well, that's funny because I thought you were all in my dream', said Ruth.

'I'm not a baboon or an orang-utang. I'm a chimpanzee, if you don't mind', said Albert.

This woke the children up very quickly as they all realised

that they were not dreaming but very much awake.

Looking out from behind the tree trunk where they had hidden, Daniel said, 'Don't hurt us!'

'I, we..', said Albert looking round at the other animals, 'we are here to help you. Don't be afraid'.

'Hurry, hurry', called some woodpeckers, who were flying and acting as lookouts, 'they are coming'.

'Get on the horses and ride away from here as fast as you can. Get to the Glassmaker's - He can help', said Albert, and with that warning the children clambered onto the still kneeling horses which then stood up and galloped off at speed.

'This is the strangest day I have ever had!', said Daniel.

'I know what you mean', replied his horse.

Ruth looked at Daniel and, despite the soldiers still chasing them, they laughed.

Jonah looked backward on his horse, 'I don't know why you are laughing - soldiers are trying to..'. He stopped talking as his horse slowed up.

The soldiers were all falling to their knees. What happened to the children started to happen to the soldiers. Soon they were all asleep on the ground.

Relieved, they got off their horses and said thank you to them, to which the horses replied that it was their pleasure and they trotted away.

Still not used to the idea of animals speaking, the children looked at one another and then turned around to continue their journey, but they found they were already there.

They were standing in front of the Glassmaker's house.

Chapter 29 - The Glassmaker's House

They stopped laughing very quickly as they were confronted by a house. This was the Glassmaker's house and now they were here they weren't very sure that they wanted to go in.

It wasn't that the cottage was frightening, or even very impressive. It was that it was the Glassmaker's house and inside there was a furnace and they were closer to the burning, hot furnace than they had ever been before.

The cottage was small and made of irregular shaped stone. It had a thatched roof and two windows painted blue and a wooden door, also painted blue. There was a short path to the front door, with green bushes and tulips on either side.

The children looked at each other and then back at the house, they moved around nervously, wondering what to do next.

Doubts started to a creep in.

'I'm not sure that this was such a good idea', said Jonah, 'Everything around here is just so strange. What if all this is a show, so that the Glassmaker can throw people into his furnace?'

Ruth said nothing as she was also scared and wondering if they should have come.

Daniel looked at them both.

'Listen, I am scared and I don't know if this is right or not but we have come so far. The river of hands, the dark gorge, the waterfall. Remember Nathaniel and how he helped us. Even the animals helped us'.

'But what if they are all in the Glassmaker's plan to throw us into the furnace', interrupted Jonah.

'Well if it is a conspiracy, it's a conspiracy of kindness and help', said Daniel.

As Daniel said this, the front door opened up by itself.

Chapter 30 - In The Entrance

The three of them stood still and were too afraid to go in. Although the door was open, the inside looked dark and frightening. They were unsure what to do. They had come so far, but they were scared. They stood looking at each other. Daniel was the first one to move. He turned towards the door and walked slowly to it.

'Daniel are you sure?', implored Jonah, who out of the three was now the least convinced that this was a good idea. In fact at that moment he would have happily started the journey home.

Daniel let out a sigh, 'Yes, we have to. I am scared, but so are our families. At least we are not prisoners. I miss them and that feeling is stronger than any fear I am feeling.' With that he continued walking through the door and disappeared from their sight.

Ruth and Jonah soon followed him into the darkness of the entrance. It took a few minutes for their eyes to adjust but when they had they found themselves in a gigantic hallway. Jonah ran out of the house again because he couldn't believe that such a big hallway could fit in the small house they had just walked into. He ran back in again.

'This is impossible. There is no way that this hallway could fit inside the cottage outside.'

Ruth reminded him what Nathaniel had said. The closer you get to the Glassmaker the more magical it became.

'I suppose it's possible. After all we have just talked to a monkey!' he replied.

'If that's true', said Daniel ,' then this must be the most magical place in the world'.

Chapter 31 - Meeting The Glassmaker

They saw that there were lots of doors going off from the enormous hallway. They went to a few of them and saw that each door had a name above it. Names such as the 'Connected Kingdom', the 'Dark World', and the 'Ice Age'. Daniel pushed the door of the one with the name 'Connected Kingdom' on it.

'Don't' said Jonah.

But it was too late. Nothing horrible happened. The opposite in fact. They saw a beautifully colourful land with many villages and people of different colours. From the doorway a river of crystal clear water flowed into each of the villages. They went to a door with the words 'Dark World' over the top but there was no handle on the door to open it.

'I'm glad there is no handle. I don't think I want to look at a place called the 'Dark World', said Ruth.

They continued to explore the great hallway until they all became aware that someone, or something, was standing behind them. They were not alone.

Their hearts were pounding and they were too nervous to move. For what seemed like an eternity, but was probably only a few seconds, nothing happened. Ruth was the first to move. She slowly turned around and screamed. What she saw was a very large person with a horrible face that had no mouth or nose at all, and he was holding a big stick. She ran as fast as she could to the door. Daniel and Jonah turned around, screamed and ran for the door as well.

'Wait. I'm so sorry, but I forgot to take my protective mask off, said the person, who was, of course, the Glassmaker. But they kept on running.

'Daniel, Ruth, Jonah, wait. Don't be afraid', said the Glassmaker,' I am so glad you have come'.

When the Glassmaker called them by name then the situation didn't seem quite so frightening. They all stopped and slowly turned around to look at the Glassmaker who had now taken off his mask.

A wonderful head of white hair fell over his shoulders and a smile so wonderful that they felt instantly at ease.

'Welcome home' said the Glassmaker.

Chapter 32 - Walking Through the Furnace

Once again, the Glassmaker reassured them.

'Don't be afraid. I will not harm you. Why should I? I made you. But you have forgotten me, and you have lived without me. I was so ready to help you, but you didn't ask. Now all of my beautiful people are broken and chipped'

The children stood in silence not sure what to say. They had heard about the Glassmaker as the creator, but they thought it was just a myth, a nice story. But now they were confronted with the fact that it was true, and that truth was quite overwhelming.

'You know my name', said Daniel.

'Yes. And I know that you are brave and kind and generous.'

'I don't feel brave or kind or generous', replied Daniel

'That's because you have forgotten; all of the things that you have been through in your life have robbed you of your identity.'

'What about our families? They are hostages and in danger. We don't know who has taken them or where they have been taken. We didn't know what to do and in desperation we came to you. Will you help us?', asked Daniel, whilst the other two remained silent, listening to every word that was being said.

For a moment the Glassmaker said nothing and the children thought he was preparing to say no.

'Of course I will help you to help them - you are my answer to their need', He eventually said

'What do you mean help us to help them? What do you mean that we are their answer? We need you to go and do it. We are all chipped and broken. We can do nothing', said Jonah, getting a bit frustrated with the Glassmaker.

The Glassmaker just smiled. Jonah found that very annoying.

'I will remake you. I will make you strong and whole.'

'How is that possible?' asked Ruth, a bit more aggressively than she had intended.

The Glassmaker calmly replied, 'By walking through the furnace.'

Chapter 33 - Choices

Jonah screamed. It was a really high pitched screamed and he was a bit embarrassed by it because it was not a very manly scream. The others looked at him.

'We have to leave NOW. Didn't you hear what He said? There is a furnace in this place and He wants to melt us down. I knew He wouldn't be good. We can rescue our families by ourselves', said Jonah in a breathless voice.

'Don't be so silly', said Ruth, angry at what Jonah was saying. She was scared at what she had heard, but didn't want to go back.

'I'm not being silly', replied Jonah and the two of them argued for a few minutes. Meanwhile Daniel had said nothing. He was deep in thought.

'I'm scared', he thought to himself, 'but what about my family. I can’t abandon them because that's what will happen if we try to rescue them by ourselves. We have no chance against whoever took them. But I don't want to go through a furnace. I don't want to be melted down. What do I do?'

The Glassmaker looked kindly on Daniel, as though He knew what he was thinking - which he did because He was the Glassmaker. Daniel looked up and saw the Glassmaker staring at him.

'Okay. I'll do it', said Daniel.

Ruth and Jonah stopped arguing and looked at Daniel, amazed at what he had just said.

Chapter 34 - Jonah Leaves

Jonah stared at Daniel, his eyebrows pushing together in disbelief.

'Are you mad?', he said, ' I thought the furnace was a joke to frighten people but now we find out it's real and you want to walk into it just because this man who we have just met asks you to? You're an idiot Daniel'.

The room was still and nobody moved after these words. Daniel and Ruth didn't move because they were embarrassed by what Jonah had said. Jonah didn't move because the words had come out more aggressively than he had intended, and he became more aware than ever of the towering presence of the Glassmaker.

The Glassmaker eventually broke the silence.

'Who do you think the shining ones are? Like Nathaniel whom you met on the road and who helped you', He asked.

They had no answer for him.

He continued,' They were people like you, who were broken and chipped and came to me because they needed help. They went through the furnace and now they are helping others and directing people to me. They were prepared to pay the cost to be made new again.'

Jonah felt very small and afraid and moved away from the Glassmaker, even though he had not been threatened in any way.

Daniel moved towards the Glassmaker.

'What do I do?' Daniel said to the Glassmaker

The Glassmaker said nothing but simply looked at a door. Above the door were two words: 'New Beginning'

Daniel moved towards the door.

Jonah shook his head and tried to stop him.

'What are you doing? You'll die and then how will you be able to help your family? He's just tricking you!'

Jonah couldn't look at the Glassmaker.

Ruth stared at Jonah.

'But what if He is telling the truth? It would change everything', and with that she walked towards Daniel.

Jonah stepped back from his friends, tears streaming down his face.

'I can't', he mumbled

He looked at the Glassmaker, and then back at his friends, and then he turned his back and walked out of the house.

Chapter 35 - Through The Furnace

Daniel and Ruth were so sad that Jonah had left.

'What will you do?' asked the Glassmaker

They said nothing, but continued towards the door.

'Together', said Daniel

'Together', said Ruth as they turned the handle and pushed the door open.

The heat that hit them was unbearable and they felt terribly afraid.

They looked at the Glassmaker, and He walked over to them and put his hands on their shoulders.

'Don't be afraid. I will be with you.'

They turned to look at the furnace, which was glowing red and orange with smoke rising from it.

Their little bodies had started to glow red because the heat was so intense, but the presence of the Glassmaker gave them courage, and so they continued despite being afraid.

They moved closer and their bodies started to glow white as they got hotter and their bodies dripped onto the ground as they started to melt. Their hearts felt as though they would explode out of their chests.

By this time, the Glassmaker had walked around to the other side of the furnace. He seemed to be unaffected by the heat.

'Just look at me', He said as they stopped in fear.

It gave them both courage to see him across the furnace and they started to walk again towards it. In all their fear a confidence started to grow. It was very strange, but they started to feel a little bit of joy. They looked at each other bewildered.

They had been holding hands and by this time their hands had melted into each other's. And still the joy grew. There was no turning back.

They were on the steps now, walking down, eyes still fixed on the Glassmaker. Their legs started to melt and they slowly fell together into the furnace.

The last thing they saw was the smiling face of the Glassmaker.

Chapter 36 - Transformation

I know that this will be terrifying to hear, but very soon there was nothing left of the two children. They had been completely melted away. But the marvellous thing is that they were still there! Even though they didn't have bodies they still existed. What made them Daniel and Ruth was still there.

They discovered that all of their fear had gone. They felt utterly peaceful, rested and safe even though they had no bodies. It was a very strange situation, but it was also a very beautiful one.

They were not quite sure what had happened or what was happening. It felt to them that they were flying even though they had no body. They laughed even though they had no mouths and they looked at each other even though they had no eyes.

'Is this it?', thought Daniel.

Ruth replied by thinking, 'No, this is just the beginning'.

They could hear each other's thoughts! They laughed again in wonder. However this time as they laughed a mouth started to form. They could feel it. Their faces started to take shape and their bodies started to be created.

Then they felt themselves start to walk out of the furnace towards the smiling face of the Glassmaker.

Chapter 37 - A New Start

They had never felt so alive before. They both ran up to the Glassmaker and embraced him. In fact they ran so fast that they knocked him over and all three rolled on the floor laughing.

Then Daniel felt an urge that he had never felt before. He felt an urge to dance and he jumped to his feet and pulled Ruth up. They held hands and they spun round and round with the Glassmaker. Breathless, the Glassmaker invited them to look at the mirror. They looked in disbelief. They had no cracks or chips. They were perfect and they were both shining ones!

Speechless, they just looked at the mirror and then the Glassmaker and then back again to the mirror.

Eventually, Daniel found some words to say.

'In a world made of glass a furnace is not the most frightening thing. A furnace is a place of hope where things can be made new.'

Daniel remembered his family. This time he did not feel helpless. He felt powerful.

He looked at Ruth, 'We must go and rescue our families.'

Ruth agreed.

They both embraced the Glassmaker.

At this time Jonah was walking through the garden. He

was getting more and more cross as he was scared, alone and felt that his friends had abandoned him. And he was angry with himself for leaving his friends.

'I must make up for leaving my friends alone with that strange furnace man', and with that thought he started to wake up the sleeping soldiers.

Chapter 38 - An Invitation To The Battle

Daniel and Ruth walked to the door that led out of the house. They looked at the Glassmaker one more time and walked through the door together. As they got outside they gasped, as they saw a huge battle going on. Shining ones, flying monsters and soldiers chasing one another and fighting each other in the air and on the ground.

The Glassmaker came and stood beside them watching them and then looking at the on-going battle.

Daniel looked at the Glassmaker.

'What is happening here?', he asked, 'What is this?'

They all stepped back as an enormous flying monster flew by, with several shining ones chasing it.

'This is the unseen battle that has been going for many years. The Shattered Lord has been trying to break glass people.'

'What must we do?' asked Ruth as she watched the battle.

The Glassmaker looked at them both with great love.

'That's up to you', He said, 'You can go and build a nice house somewhere and settle down. Or you can fight'.

The Glassmaker didn't look at them but stared in the distance.

Daniel and Ruth looked at each other, knowing the answer, but nervous.

'We will fight.'

The Glassmaker smiled.

'I will always be with you. I will never leave you.'

Daniel was just about to reply to the Glassmaker when a shining one, who had been in the midst of the battle that had always been going on ran up to them and said, 'Come and fight for the glory of the Glassmaker'.

TO BE CONTINUED IN
'THE GLASS PEOPLE AND THE GREAT RESCUE'

Book II
The Glass People and the Great Rescue

Alan Kilpatrick

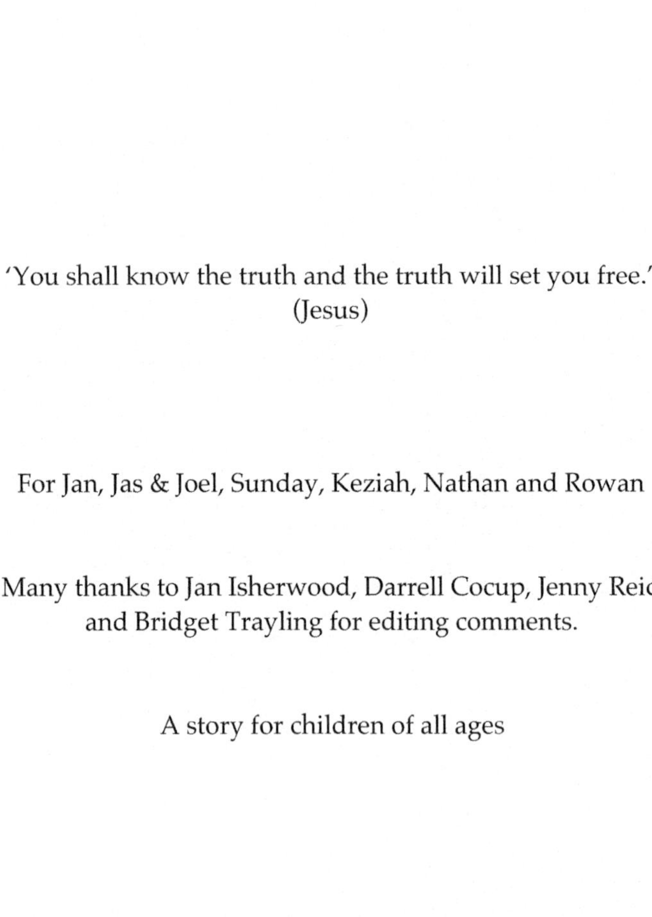

'You shall know the truth and the truth will set you free.'
(Jesus)

For Jan, Jas & Joel, Sunday, Keziah, Nathan and Rowan

Many thanks to Jan Isherwood, Darrell Cocup, Jenny Reid and Bridget Trayling for editing comments.

A story for children of all ages

Chapter 1 - Daniel and Ruth see the battle for the first time

Daniel and Ruth were overwhelmed. Not just by what had just happened to them, but also by what they now saw. It was as though someone had taken a blank canvas and had splattered different colours of paint over it, with no thought as to where the paint went. Shining ones were running and battling with soldiers who were dull grey. Monsters, like the one they had glimpsed in the sky after coming out of the snowy chasm, were flying with grey soldiers on their backs. They were swooping and diving after the shining ones. Sparks of brilliant light exploded all around as shining ones wielded their swords against their enemies.

In addition to all of this, Daniel and Ruth were trying to come to terms with the fact that they had been completely transformed and had been put back together when they had walked through the Glassmaker's furnace. They had once thought that in a world made of glass, a furnace was the most frightening thing. They now knew that was wrong. In a world made of glass, a furnace is a place of hope where things can be made new. They had no more cracks or fractures on their bodies. As well as coming to terms with the sight that they were now shining ones, they were also coming to terms with the sense of joy, peace and courage they both felt growing within them. Daniel was no longer scared or frustrated with Ruth. He felt strong and courageous. Ruth felt peaceful and focussed. They examined each other. They both looked different, but they could still recognise one another.

Their families had been captured by mysterious soldiers and their village had been burnt to the ground. They didn't know what to do. They had heard of the Glassmaker but didn't know if He was real or not. So Daniel, Ruth and their friend Jonah, had journeyed to the Glassmaker's house to discover the truth. They found out that He was real and that He was good. They discovered that the truth was more wonderful than they could have ever imagined. But Jonah hadn't trusted him and he had ran out of the house, leaving them both with the Glassmaker. They didn't know where he was or what had happened to him. They trusted the Glassmaker and He had made them whole when they had walked through the furnace. They had surrendered everything to him and they had been transformed. Now they stood, completely transformed, watching a battle and thinking about their families and Jonah.

They turned towards the Glassmaker who was watching the chaotic scene.

Daniel was about to ask him something when a shining one rushed up to them and shouted, 'Come and fight for the glory of the Glassmaker'.

Ruth and Daniel looked at each other and then smiled.

Ruth said, 'We don't want to settle down somewhere and build a house. Too much has happened to us and our families are still imprisoned. We will fight!'

The shining one, whose name was Noah, laughed as he dodged a flying monster and drove his sword into its side as it passed him. The monster screamed as it lost all control and hit the ground. It didn't move again.

'One day, soon', the Glassmaker said, 'I am coming to change everything and the Shattered Lord will be broken to pieces. All will be made right. But there will be a cost and there will be a sacrifice. You will be tested. In those times remember these words: I am coming again. Now go and fight and be strong and courageous'.

Daniel and Ruth ran to the Glassmaker and embraced him.

'Thank you for making us whole again', said Daniel and with that Daniel and Ruth both ran after Noah.

They entered the battle that had been going on but never seen, and they didn't look back.

They didn't see the flying monster with the grey soldier on its back racing towards them.

Chapter 2 - A close escape!

Daniel and Ruth started to follow Noah. As they ran they had to jump over grey soldiers who had been defeated by the shining ones. It was a terrible sight. They glimpsed some of the faces of the soldiers who lay still on the ground and saw that their features had softened to become like a simple glass person. The grey soldiers had once been just like them. What had happened to them? Why were they fighting for the Shattered Lord?

They became aware of voices shouting at them, but they couldn't make out the words. In the distance, they saw several shining ones, who were hidden in a depression in the land, mouthing words at them. Daniel and Ruth couldn't hear them. However, they understood the fingers pointing behind them and the eyes glancing from them to whatever was behind.

They all turned around and saw the danger approaching at a high speed. The flying monster was hideous. From a distance, Daniel and Ruth couldn't make out any features on it. As it closed in on them they could see that it had glass splinters falling from its body as it flew and it looked like a huge flying cat.

The noise grew as it drew near to them. The noise of the flapping wings. The noise of the splintered glass hitting the ground. The noise of the monster's screech. The noise of the grey soldier sitting on top of the creature shouting at the creature to go faster.

They ran as fast as they could as the flying monster approached. In their haste, Daniel tripped over one of the fallen soldiers and fell flat on his face.

Ruth and Noah stopped running and turned to help Daniel.

'Daniel', shouted Ruth.

'Run', yelled Daniel, 'I'm okay'. He got up and ran, but the monster had gained ground on them. It was closer than ever.

'Over here', cried the shining ones that had pointed out the danger behind them. They were frantically waving at them to come over to where they were.

Daniel, Ruth and Noah all raced towards the shouting shining ones.

At that moment all seemed to go into slow motion. The flying monster was on top of them. Noah stopped running and turned around. He lay on his back with his sword pointing upwards just as the flying monster caught up with them. It roared as Noah's sword caught its underbelly. The awful creature spiralled out of control and landed with a thunderous crash on the ground between Daniel, Ruth and Noah and the safety of the other shining ones.

Their way was blocked by the beast, but their momentum enabled them to jump over the flying monster, just as another one made its attack. They barely escaped the second flying monster and slid down the bank of the hollow and crashed into the shining ones. They ended on the ground laughing, as the battle continued around them.

Chapter 3 - Beginnings 1

In the beginning, the Glassmaker blew life into the various glass creatures that He had created. Soft molten glass was soon moulded into beautiful spheres of shimmering colours that floated in the air like countless stars in the sky. The Glassmaker took each of the spheres and started to shape them into unique glass creatures. The forms of different animals began to appear. Some frightening to look at and some beautiful.

A huge company of spirit beings made of glass watched on as the Glassmaker shaped the formless glass into things they had never seen before. The Glassmaker sang as He created. The animals walked around and looked at each other and the spirit beings. The Glassmaker's furnace room became louder and louder with the noise of so many different animals. Barks and roars, squeaks and squeals, twitters and chirping, baying and neighs.

When it looked like the Glassmaker had finished, He rubbed his hands together, looked at the spirit beings and said, 'Now for the people'. The spirit beings looked at each other.

'What's a "people"?', one asked another.

'Haven't a clue', came the reply, 'But we will soon find out'.

The company of spirit beings gathered closer to watch 'people' being made.

One who stood close to the Glassmaker was a being called Ramiel. He was one of the Glassmaker's most trusted and loyal advisors.

As they all watched, they witnessed a growing army of 'people'. The spirit beings eyes opened wider and wider as they realised that the 'people' looked just like the Glassmaker. In time a vast army of 'people' stood before them all. Motionless. Lifeless.

Mumblings and chatter started to rise from the spirit beings.

'What has He made?' said one.

'Does He not need us anymore?' echoed another.

Some just exclaimed, 'Why?'.

Ramiel looked around, concerned.

The Glassmaker, hearing the mumbling and worries, just smiled.

That was not the end of the creation of the 'glass people'. The Glassmaker walked up to the company of motionless people, and one by one He held their heads, looked into the lifeless eyes and breathed his breath into them.

Warmth and colour emanated from the body of each glass person as they breathed for the first time, saw through their eyes for the first time and smiled at their Glassmaker.

All of the spirit beings stepped forward in amazement.

Tabbris, an aide of Ramiel, leant towards Ramiel and asked, 'What is He doing?'

Ramiel said nothing, but his eyes moved around his head as though he was searching for answers.

Tabbris demanded an answer, 'What is He doing?'

Under his breath Ramiel replied fiercely, 'I don't know!'

Tabbris stepped back, intimidated by the anger of his superior. Ramiel fixed his gaze once more on the Glassmaker and stared at him. On the outside, Ramiel looked calm, but on the inside, he was feeling things that he had never felt before. He was angry. He was angry at the Glassmaker, at the 'glass people'. Ramiel had been created just like the 'glass people', but the Glassmaker had never held Ramiel by the face and breathed on him.

'Is this jealousy?', he thought to himself.

Chapter 4 - Jonah meets the grey soldiers

Jonah ran out of the Glassmaker's house into the garden, tears streaming down his face.

He was so sad that he had to leave his friends. Was he the only sensible one? He had to try and save them from the Glassmaker. They had been tricked! How could they have been so foolish?

'I must do something' he thought to himself.

As he ran into the garden and away from the house, he tripped over something and landed flat on his face.

'Ow', he cried as his nose was yet again broken off. His nose was hanging on by the tape he had used before. He fixed his nose and slowly regained his composure. He looked back to where he had tripped and saw what it was that had got in his way.

'No', he shouted as he realised that he had stumbled over a grey soldier. He stood up and ran as quickly as he could away from the sleeping soldiers, for there was more than one.

'Leave me alone', he cried out in despair, thinking that they were now chasing him. He looked over his shoulders as he was running to see if the soldiers were closing on him. As he did so he saw that they hadn't stirred, but remained sleeping on the ground. He slowed down, still moving away from them. Was this a trap? Nothing moved. The soldiers stayed on the ground sleeping. He looked around to see if any were hiding behind trees and bushes, ready to pounce on him. Everything was still and silent.

He stopped running and stood in the silent garden. Waiting to see if anything happened. But nothing did.

He was puzzled, his face scrunched up as he tried to work out what was going on.

He started to take a step back to the soldiers. Slowly one step and then another, continuously looking around still thinking it could be a trap. Suddenly, movement came from one of the trees. His heart raced. It was just a bird. The soldiers lay sleeping.

'Calm yourself', he spoke out loud, hoping that the sound of his own voice would make him less scared and lonely.

At last, he was standing over them.

'Maybe they could help me?', he thought foolishly, and with that silly thought, he prodded a soldier nearby with his foot. The soldier slept on. Feeling brave, he kicked a little harder. This time a groan came from the soldier. Then, the soldier started to move and got to his feet. Jonah kicked the others and one by one by one they got up and stretched the sleep away, yawning as they did so.

The first soldier Jonah had woken was now coming back to his senses. He looked at Jonah.

'Who are you?', he said gruffly.

'Jonah, and you must help me'.

'Must I?', replied the soldier, laughing and looking at the other soldiers.

'Yes you must - my friends have been captured by the Glassmaker. He has bewitched them and he is going to melt them down. I must stop him. Please help', Jonah demanded.

'Not likely', said another of the soldier, 'We're not stepping foot inside that house'.

'Your friends are gone', said another.

'No, no, no', yelled Jonah, 'That's not true!'

Jonah started to become uneasy as he sensed that the soldiers were gathering around him. Trapping him.

'What are you doing?' he said in a shaky voice.

'The first solider, who seemed to be in charge, said, 'We lost the other two, but we have you. We're your new friends now!'

'I'm not your friend. I just need your help!'

'Oh, you're too good for us. Is that what you're saying?' said the soldier in charge.

'No, of course not', said Jonah, trying to back out of the decreasing circle of soldiers.

'You're one of us', said another one of the soldiers.

'No I am not!' shouted Jonah.

'Yes you are', laughed the soldiers.

'Take a look at yourself', they said.

'What do you mean', replied Jonah, a sense of dread washing over him. Jonah looked into the eyes of each of the grey soldiers. Then slowly he looked at himself. His arms, his hands, his legs, his body had all turned grey. He looked just like the grey soldiers!

Chapter 5 - Daniel and Ruth make new friends and learn a horrible truth

Daniel, Ruth and Noah ducked as the second flying monster swooped over their heads chasing another shining one.

They remained on the ground, recovering their breath. The troops that had helped them stood looking and smiling at them.

One of them walked up to Noah, put out her hand and pulled Noah to his feet. They embraced.

'This is Daniel and this is Ruth', he said to the soldier who had helped him up, 'They have just gone through the Glassmaker's furnace and are brand new!'

The shining ones cheered and went to help Daniel and Ruth to their feet, welcoming and embracing them as they did so.

'I'm Jade', said the soldier who had helped Noah, 'and this is Ranger and his sister Firestone'. Ranger and Firestone smiled at Daniel and Ruth.

'And this is our leader Noah', Jade continued, pointing to the soldier who had called Daniel and Ruth to the battle.

Noah smiled. Daniel looked around at the battle that was raging about them.

'Don't worry', said Noah, 'We are safe here for the

moment. Where are you from?'

Daniel and Ruth looked at each other. Daniel nodded to Ruth and she told their tale.

'We are from a small village called Knock', she said.

'We heard what happened there', said Jade.

'Everything is gone, Everything was taken. Including our families. That is why we went on our journey to the Glassmaker's house. We didn't even know if He was good or bad or if He even existed. We were desperate and had no-one else to go to', continued Ruth.

Ruth was getting emotional as she thought of her family. She paused thinking of her mother and father. As Daniel sat quietly remembering, she continued telling their story.

'There were three of us that started the journey. Jonah, our friend...'. Ruth's voice faltered as she remembered Jonah. Daniel could see that she wasn't going to finish the sentence.

'Jonah refused to go through the furnace. He said that we were being tricked and that the Glassmaker was not good', said Daniel, ending the story Ruth had started.

Firestone spoke up for the first time. She was tall and had a faint reddish glow about her.

'We all have family and friends who refused to trust the Glassmaker. But never doubt', she said looking at Daniel and Ruth, 'that the Glassmaker is good - always'.

'What happens to those who don't go through the furnace?' asked Daniel almost too afraid to ask the question.

No-one spoke. At last, Ranger pointed to the grey soldiers.

Daniel and Ruth both closed their eyes, pain etched on their faces.

'Oh Jonah', whispered Ruth

Daniel opened his eyes and looked at Noah.

'What about the flying monsters? What are they?' he asked

'They are called Splinter Cats and in ages past, they used to serve the Glassmaker. They were a little like us, but jealousy entered them and fractured their hearts. Over time the outside became like the inside and changed the way they looked. They have poison in their tails and they now serve the Shattered Lord.', answered Noah.

At the mention of the Shattered Lord Daniel and Ruth, both said at the same time, 'Who?' They looked at each other, smiled and looked back at Noah.

'The Shattered Lord is the reason for all of the brokenness and fractures in our world. He was, a very long time ago, one of the Glassmakers closest advisors. Legend has it that when the Glassmaker created the Glass Kingdom and all of its people, jealousy entered into his heart and the first fracture happened. He then led a revolt against the Glassmaker. But he lost that battle and he and all the rebels were cast out of the Glassmaker's presence. He has tried to destroy the Glass Kingdom and all of its people ever since', said Noah.

He stopped talking and looked at the others as though he was avoiding saying something.

'What is it?' asked Ruth, an uneasiness rising up within her.

Noah hesitated.

'What is it?' asked Ruth, this time with more urgency in her voice.

'Unless they choose to serve him, all of those taken prisoner by the Shattered Lord, including your families, are melted down', said Noah.

Chapter 6 - Daniel, Ruth and the troop of shining ones are given an assignment

Daniel and Ruth cried out and wept as they heard what might have happened to their families.

'We must go and rescue them! Now!' shouted Daniel.

Ruth stood by his side saying nothing, but obviously agreeing with the idea.

'We know how you feel' said Ranger, 'Firestone and I both saw our parents die at the hand of the Shattered Lord.'

'They were melted down in front of us,' continued Firestone, 'We managed to escape and ran to the Glassmaker's house'.

'All of my family were taken just like yours', said Jade, 'I don't know whether they are alive or have been melted.'

'We need to try and see if all our families are alive', Ruth said to Jade.

'Will you help us?', asked Daniel

At this point, the largest and mightiest shining one Daniel and Ruth had seen flew up to them all.

Noah, Jade, Firestone and Ranger all saluted.

'I see you have two new recruits', boomed the shining one — who was called Michael.

'Yes sir', Replied Noah.

'The Glassmaker has an assignment for you all. He wants you to go to the shattered castle and find out how many glass people are imprisoned there.' said Michael.

The small gathering looked at one another recognising the honour of being asked, but also aware of the sacrifice that was being asked.

'The Glassmaker wants you to take the new recruits with you', said Michael,' They have an important role to play in this battle'.

'Yes sir', said Noah, 'But sir, the desert…'.

He stopped talking as he saw that Michael was not going to change the plan.

'Yes, sir,' they all said.

Michael looked at Daniel and Ruth. He smiled at them.

'Don't be afraid. The Glassmaker is with you. When you can't go forward, kneel and ask for help,' he said to them and with that he flew off.

'Why are you so hesitant?' asked Daniel, 'We must do what he says!'

'It's not that easy,' said Jade, 'We have to go through the desert'.

'What desert? What is so bad about them?' said Ruth.

Noah answered, 'The desert is a place of testing that you have to go through to get to the Shattered Lord's castle. Many have tried to go through them, but they were never seen again. If you fail in the desert you will stay in the desert — forever.'

Chapter 7 - Jonah tries to escape, and hidden onlookers

Jonah tried to run. He thought if he ran quickly he might leave the grey colour behind and he would return to his normal glass colour. He couldn't accept the fact that he was grey. It was just not possible. Why was he grey when all he had done was try and help his friends?

He didn't get far. Two of the grey soldiers, now fully awake, ran after him and caught him roughly.

'Where do you think you're going?', said one. The two soldiers carried Jonah back to the others with Jonah wriggling and kicking out trying to escape.

'Leave me alone!' he demanded.

This just made the soldiers more amused.

'Wriggle and kick all you want. You are going nowhere', said the soldier who seemed to be in charge. He put his face right up to Jonah's and, as he spoke, spit fell on Jonah's face. Jonah turned his face away, tried to escape the spit. A tear started to run down his cheek.

The sergeant of the grey soldiers noticed it.

'Aw, that is so sweet. Missing your friends?' mocked the sergeant.

This just made Jonah more determined to escape. But it

was no use. He hung limply in the arms of his captors, tears starting to flow.

'I just wanted to help my friends', he said to himself, 'I still need to help my friends'. The conviction in his voice was changing. He was not so sure that his friends had made the wrong choice. But maybe they were dead. At least he was alive, even if he was grey.

'Come on lads. Tie him up and let's take him to the Shattered Lord's castle', ordered the sergeant.

Jonah looked at him.

'You don't know who he is, do you? The Shattered Lord', asked the sergeant.

Jonah shook his head and let it drop in despair.

'Oh, you are in for a real treat', said the sergeant laughing at Jonah's plight.

Chapter 8 - Jonah denies he is grey and escapes

As Jonah was being mocked and tied up, hidden in the trees and bushes, animals watched what was happening. They all talked, because the closer you get to the Glassmaker the more magical things become.

Albert (who was a chimpanzee and not a baboon or orang-utang) watched the unfolding scene.

'No, no no', he said, 'this was not supposed happen!'

'What are we going to do?', asked one of the horses, who was called Zeus.

'We need to do something', said a wolf named Fleck.

'Yes, I know', said Albert, his gaze still fixed on Jonah. Albert then looked up at an owl in the tree.

'What do you think we should do, Oswald?', he asked

The owl turned his head completely around and stared at Albert with big wide eyes.

'We need to go to Pinecone Woods. Jonah cannot be helped at the moment without endangering all the other animals. We need to help Daniel and Ruth. They are the key to success and, after they have gone through the testing, they will go through Pinecone Woods. It is there that we can really start to help', said Oswald.

With that said, all the animals watched as Jonah was chained by his hands and feet and dragged off to the castle of the Shattered Lord.

The grey soldiers were very rough with Jonah. Cracks started to appear on his wrists and ankles where the chains bit in. He felt very sad and tired and just wanted to lie down and sleep. All that had happened and was happening to him was too much for him to deal with. He wanted to shut it all out by simply closing his eyes. However, he knew that closing his eyes wouldn't really change anything.

'I am not grey. I am not grey', he repeated to himself over and over again.

One of the soldiers overheard him and came right up to Jonah's ear.

'Oh yes, you are my matey. You're as grey as they come', he whispered.

Jonah snapped and tried to hit the soldier, but the chains wouldn't allow him to. The soldier jumped back forgetting that Jonah couldn't touch him. When the soldier realised this, he started laughing at Jonah and walked away.

Anger started to rise up within Jonah and he determined to escape. But how? He looked at his chains and realised that it was impossible. The choice he made at the Glassmaker's House had become his prison.

Chapter 9 - Beginnings 2

The Glassmaker had continued to create more and more glass people. He started to create and shape the glass world in which they would live. The newly created glass people ran into their new home with joy and laughter. The spirit beings continued to look on in amazement at what was happening.

A group of spirit beings made their way over to Ramiel.

'We are not happy with what is happening', said one to Ramiel.

'Why is He doing this?', said another.

'What are you going to do about it, Ramiel?', said a third.

All conversation stopped in the little group that had gathered around Ramiel and all eyes were fixed on him.

'I'm going to talk to him, ask him what this is all about', said Ramiel.

Ramiel requested a meeting with the Glassmaker and he entered the simple workshop in which the Glassmaker spent most of his time. In the middle of the room, a large furnace constantly burned. In this, the glass had been melted down to create the newly formed glass people.

The Glassmaker became aware that Ramiel was there and He took off his large protective mask.

'Ramiel, welcome, welcome, welcome! I am so glad you

are here!'

'You are?' said Ramiel

'Of course, I am. Do you doubt that I love being with you?' replied the Glassmaker.

Ramiel ignored the question and got straight to the point.

'Why did you create the glass people? Weren't we enough for you?' he asked the Glassmaker.

The Glassmaker took in a deep breath and sighed.

'Am I not enough for you?' the Glassmaker asked Ramiel.

Ramiel knew he should say, 'of course you are', but he didn't feel it in his heart. He felt a hardness start to invade his spirit. The hardness felt like anger.

Ramiel became aware that his fist was tightly clenched. The tension in his hand was so strong that a tiny crack appeared in the palm of his hand.

Chapter 10 - Jonah is imprisoned in the castle

It was a long journey to the Shattered Lord's castle. They could walk through the desert easily because it was under the authority of the Shattered Lord. Jonah was dragged most of the way. At first, he resisted walking and the soldiers pulled him along. Later, he was so weary he could hardly walk and then the soldiers hauled him along the ground.

He was hurting outside and inside. His body ached from being heaved along the ground. His inside ached because he realised that he had abandoned his friends and may have made the wrong decision.

The castle was a huge dark place, with prison cells all along the outside, with the prisoners visible to anyone approaching. They called and cried for his help, but he felt as though he was the one who needed help.

As he entered the Castle itself he saw a long line of people being ushered unwillingly into a doorway. As he passed the doorway, he realised that the glowing orange light that came from the room beyond contained a furnace.

He struggled to escape, thinking he was being taken to the furnace.

'Steady on, boy. It's not your time', said the sergeant and pushed Jonah onwards.

'Wh...wh..what's happening in there? What do you mean

it's not my time?' Jonah uttered in fear.

'You'll find out soon enough', said another of the soldiers.

Jonah was led, reluctantly, into a wing of the Castle that contained many cells. They led him up a rickety staircase and then shoved him into one of the cells, and then left him alone.

'Wait! Help me!', Jonah cried, but no one was listening.

He turned around and saw that he was very high up in a cell in the Castle wall. He looked out in the broken surroundings of the Castle. He crumpled to his knees, let his head fall back and yelled in desperation, alone and cold.

Chapter 11 - Daniel and Ruth head to the desert

The words, 'If you fail in the desert you will stay in the desert - forever' were still echoing around Daniel's head.

Ruth was looking at him as they walked towards the desert knowing what he was worried about.

'We have to try - even if we do fail', she said to Daniel, 'Our families need us to try'.

'I know', retorted Daniel.

He stopped and looked at Ruth realising he had spoken angrily to her.

'I'm sorry. I didn't mean to be cross at you. I am just afraid of failing. I'm not worried about what will happen to me, but my family are counting on me', he said more gently to her.

They continued to walk, following Noah and the rest of the troop.

After what seemed like the longest walk the terrain started to change and became rockier. Eventually, the rocks became smaller and smaller, until Daniel and Ruth found themselves standing at the edge of a vast desert.

The wind was blowing the sand around and it was difficult to see very far. After a time the wind died down and the view cleared.

It seemed like there was no end to the desert. It stretched

out forever.

'How are we going to cross this?', said Daniel

'Step by step', said Ranger.

'And test by test', continued Firestone

Ruth had not taken her gaze from the desert.

'What are you staring at?' asked Daniel, trying to follow her gaze.

'I don't know. Look in the distance there seems to be lots of large rocks. What are they?', she replied.

Sure enough, in the distance, there were what looked like large white rocks, in no regular pattern all across the desert. The rocks were, of course, completely motionless, but at the same time, there seemed to be a shimmering movement coming from them. Each rock was a different shape from the one next to it. They looked like mirages.

Noah answered Ruth.

'They are not rocks. The truth is they are shining ones who have tried to cross the desert. They have failed the test and have been stuck in the desert. Some have been stuck for many, many years. We are all going to be faced with the same choices!'

Chapter 12 - The start of the desert testing

'What will happen when we step onto the desert?', asked Ruth. She was asking, not in order to find out, but to delay the moment when they would have to move into the desert. It wasn't something she really wanted to do, although she knew that she must.

'We don't know. We have never been into the desert before', said Noah, 'When you go into the desert you either get out on the other side or you get stuck in it. There is no coming back. No one has come back so we don't know what happens in it. All we know is that there are times of testing ahead'.

Those words increased the sombre mood of the troop.

It was Daniel who moved first.

'We can't stand here all day. Let's go', he said

He grabbed Ruth's hand and with that, they walked into the desert.

Noah, Jade, Ranger and Firestone watched as the forms of Daniel and Ruth turned from being solid into shimmering outlines of shining ones. They were moving so slowly that it looked as though they were standing still.

The four experienced soldiers looked at each other and walked into the desert.

* * *

To the soldiers who stood by the edge of the desert, it looked as though Daniel and Ruth were barely moving. To Daniel and Ruth, everything moved at lightning speed. They moved so fast and with such force that it felt as though they would be broken apart from each other and from within. Suddenly, everything stopped. They looked around and saw that they were near other shining ones. They tried to call to them, but either they couldn't be heard or the other shining ones didn't want to listen. Daniel and Ruth tried to reach out to them. They could almost touch them at first, but the longer they were there, the further the shining ones moved away. Very soon every shining one in the desert was moving away from each other. Not that they were moving away through choice. Every object in the desert was being isolated from everything else.

Daniel and Ruth held each other's hands tighter as they involuntarily moved away from everything else until they were completely and utterly alone in the desert.

Chapter 13 - Beginnings 3

Ramiel clenched his fist tighter to try and hide the small crack in his hand, but as he did so the crack became bigger. The crack was audible and the Glassmaker looked at Ramiel.

'Is everything alright Ramiel?', asked the Glassmaker

'Yes, of course, it is', replied Ramiel tersely, putting his cracked hand behind his back.

'I still can't understand why you created the glass people. We are your loyal servants. We can do everything you require!', continued Ramiel

'Yes, you could', said the Glassmaker thoughtfully, 'But isn't it good to bring others into the joy of living?'

'Well, yes I suppose so. But, isn't it better to concentrate on those you have and make sure you have enough to give to those who already live?', said Ramiel.

The Glassmaker smiled. 'There is always more than enough! Life doesn't run out. Neither do I', He said.

Ramiel thought about this for a moment and found himself getting increasingly frustrated.

'Don't you see that your goodness is upsetting those who already live. They don't understand what is happening and they are getting nervous that you are forgetting them!' said Ramiel, his voice getting louder.

'They don't need to understand', answered the

Glassmaker, 'They just need to trust'

'You don't understand', shouted Ramiel, 'Again, I repeat, if you have them, then why on earth do you need us. In fact, if you have them to serve you then why do I need to serve you! What's the point!'

With those words, the crack in Ramiel's hand spread up to his elbow.

Chapter 14 - Daniel and Ruth's first challenge

'What now?' asked Ruth, looking around at the nothingness that surrounded them.

'Where's the desert?' replied Daniel.

'I don't know', responded Ruth, 'It seems to have disappeared.'

Time seemed more real. They felt time passing with a presence they had never experienced before. The way they felt it passing was the hunger and tiredness that grew within them. They slept and woke up hungry so many times. They felt every moment.

After countless moments, Ruth looked around and something in the far distance caught her gaze.

'I am so…', started Daniel and then stopped as he noticed Ruth staring at an object far away. He followed her gaze to the object.

'What is that?', he whispered.

As he spoke the object grew larger and came closer to them, even though they were not moving. They looked at each other, stood up and tried to run away from the object.

They kept looking over their shoulders to see how far away they were getting, but it was no use, as the object was gaining and overtook them and stopped immediately in front of them.

The object looked like an enormous tree. It had a light brown trunk, and where the branches and leaves should have been, there was a large cloud-like structure that was a deep brown and looked as though it had been carved out of a very big piece of wood.

Daniel and Ruth looked at each other and, then, back at the tree. All was still and silent and they both felt very uneasy. They started taking small steps away from the tree.

Suddenly, hundreds of pairs of eyes appeared in the tree cloud, all looking directly at Daniel and Ruth.

Daniel and Ruth panicked and backed off more quickly.

'Where do you think you are going?' boomed a voice out of nowhere and as the voice echoed, the tree cloud structure transformed into many brown spheres with eyes. They rolled off the top of the trunk and surrounded Daniel and Ruth. Large thorns appeared all over the spheres and large, yellow eyes watched them. Daniel and Ruth were trapped!

Chapter 15 - Daniel and Ruth speak to the first tree

It was not the spheres that had spoken, but it was the tree trunk. Branches had appeared when the spheres had trapped Daniel and Ruth and it looked now like a tree in the Wintertime, like a tree skeleton.

Daniel and Ruth had raised their swords and were standing back to back, circling around trying to find a way through.

'It's very sweet to watch you think about escape. There is no way through, of course', said the voice from the tree trunk.

Daniel and Ruth continued to circle and think about escape.

'Who are you?', asked Daniel, 'and why have you trapped us?'

'I am the first tree. I have been here for so very long and I just love company. Will you stay with me?', answered the tree.

'Why on earth should we stay with you?', said Ruth.

'Because I am the first tree. I can give you what you want', came the reply.

'What do you think we want?', asked Daniel, his voice raspy through lack of water.

'I can give you food and water', said the first tree.

Daniel and Ruth looked at each other.

'To have the water you simply need to serve me for a time', continued the first tree.

'Why don't you just give us the food and water? Isn't that the kind thing to do?', said Ruth

The first tree laughed and the ground shook.

'No', said Daniel quietly at first, 'No, we will not serve you! We are the Glassmaker's children! You shouldn't need to force people to serve you!'

With those words, everything changed. The first tree exploded and they looked on a different scene. They were in prison!

Chapter 16 - Beginnings 4

The crack in Ramiel's arm was obvious to the Glassmaker and so Ramiel turned and walked away from the Glassmaker.

'Why are you going?', asked the Glassmaker.

'Why should I stay?', replied Ramiel.

'Don't you want to be with me? Do I not give you joy?', said the Glassmaker, 'Turn around and look at me Ramiel'.

Ramiel paused but didn't turn around. He kept his back to the Glassmaker.

There was a heaviness in Ramiel. He could sense it and the Glassmaker could see it.

In the silence of the room, the newly created glass people could be heard laughing and talking.

'Who will rule the Glass Kingdom?' asked Ramiel, 'Who will have authority over them?'

'What a strange question to ask, Ramiel. You know that they will have no other king than me', said the Glassmaker.

'It's not strange at all', said Ramiel with a rasping voice, 'You are probably going to put them in charge of us and make us serve them!'

'Do you not want to serve others?', answered the Glassmaker

'Not them', said Ramiel quietly, so the Glassmaker couldn't hear.

The jealousy that had been born in Ramiel when the glass people were first created, was now starting to take root in his heart. He could feel the tentacles of envy wrap themselves around his heart and he started to feel a coldness towards the Glassmaker. He had never felt that before. It frightened him, but it also excited him.

'Give me more power', he said quietly

The Glassmaker said nothing.

Ramiel turned slightly towards the Glassmaker, a disrespectful boldness coming over him.

'Give me more power', he repeated more loudly, 'Give me more power and I will rule the glass people!'

The crack in his arm lengthened and stretched up his neck and started to move over his face, deforming his once gentle and loving features.

Chapter 17 - Daniel and Ruth's second challenge

It was dark and cold in the prison cell and they could hear people crying. Their eyes started to adjust to the darkness and, soon they could make out the forms of people and, then the faces.

'Mother! Father!', cried out Daniel and ran over to his family.

Ruth looked on in astonishment and then recognised her own family and likewise ran over to them.

Daniel's mother and father stood up and cowered in the corner as Daniel ran to them.

"Get away from us!', he shouted at Daniel.

'What do you mean?', said Daniel, 'It's me, Daniel, your son!'

'No, you are not', said his father, 'Daniel is dead. I don't know you. Leave us alone!'.

Daniel moved towards them, but an invisible barrier prevented him from going near his parents. He pushed with all his strength to get to his family, but the barrier stopped him. Even if he had gotten through, his family didn't recognise him or want him.

Ruth had the same experience with her family. The shining warriors stood side by side, holding hands and weeping with sorrow. Here they were with their families, but their families didn't recognise them.

'It's so sad, isn't it?', said the voice in the darkness.

Daniel and Ruth looked around in the direction of the voice, knowing it was the first tree.

The tree moved forward on its roots, and Daniel and Ruth both ran towards it. They wanted to hurt it. To cause it pain. They knew that the tree was the reason for their families not recognising them. As soon as they got near the tree it simply disappeared and reappeared somewhere else in the prison cell.

After countless attempts to harm the tree, Daniel and Ruth were too tired to continue. Their families rejecting them had enraged them to attack the first tree. The realisation that they couldn't harm it had sapped all the fight from them. They both sank to the ground, exhausted and defeated.

'Serve me and I will take the blindness from your families. They will recognise you and you can be a family again', said the tree.

'I hate you!', cried Ruth and made one more attempt to hurt the tree. One more time she failed.

She fell to the floor, helpless and in pain.

'I want my family!', she said, tears rolling from her cheeks onto the floor, 'I just want my family.'

Daniel went to her and put his arm around her.

'This can all be over. You can be with them now. Serve me. It's such a simple thing to do', implored the first tree, 'Isn't that what you want?'

Ruth spoke, weakly, 'Yes, but not this way. We are the Glassmaker's children!'

The room darkened until it felt as though the darkness was a physical thing wrapping itself around Ruth and Daniel. It felt heavy. Suddenly, light exploded all around them. Daniel and Ruth were sitting on two thrones.

Chapter 18 - Beginnings 5

Ramiel twisted his head slightly in discomfort as the crack spread over his face.

The Glassmaker knew what was starting to happen. He had known from the very start. He could not force Ramiel into a different path, though he could love him into different choices.

'Ramiel', called the Glassmaker gently.

Ramiel turned his back once more on the Glassmaker, thinking that in doing so the Glassmaker could not see the cracks on his body.

He started to shield his eyes. The light from the Glassmaker was starting to blind him, starting to annoy him. He had never been aware that the Glassmaker shone so brightly. Ramiel was unaware that the light he carried had started to fade and a greyness was enfolding him.

Tabbris, Ramiel's aide, quietly entered the room and stared at Ramiel.

'What is happening to you?', he asked Ramiel, and looking at the Glassmaker 'What have you done to him?'

'Yes, that's it Tabbris, look at what the illustrious Glassmaker has done to me. He just stands there, inflicting suffering on me, preferring his newly created glass people over those who have served him for so many years', said

Ramiel, getting into a flow of speaking and gaining confidence.

'Maybe the plan is to get rid of us, to do away with us', continued Ramiel.

Tabbris stood quietly, shocked at how Ramiel was talking to the Glassmaker, but even more shocked that the Glassmaker seemed to be doing nothing. He might even be causing Ramiel pain. Ramiel looked so changed, so different from Tabbris. So dull compared to his previous brightness. So broken.

'Please stop hurting him', Tabbris cried out to the Glassmaker.

Still, the Glassmaker did nothing, but watch.

'If you are not doing away with us, then give me more power!', demanded Ramiel, 'Let me rule over the glass people instead of you. Let me have my own throne! Then, I will believe you!'

At that moment the ground started to shake, the Glassmaker started to shine even brighter and grew until He filled the room with His presence.

Chapter 19 - Daniel and Ruth's third challenge

Thousands of people were gathered around the thrones that Daniel and Ruth were sitting on. The first tree stood near them. The people were calling out their names, King Daniel and Queen Ruth, over and over again. The atmosphere of love and adoration was intoxicating and Daniel and Ruth smiled despite themselves.

The thorny spheres were positioned around the thrones and let only privileged guests come to the foot of the thrones one at a time. Each guest smiled at the King and Queen and lay gifts at their feet. The wine was brought and Daniel and Ruth drank deeply as they were thirsty and ate the food that was brought to them. The first tree laid out a feast for them and only asked that they enjoy. This was their kingdom, he said, and he would always be near them to guide them.

Time passed, and each moment Daniel and Ruth received love and honour from the people. They drank and ate and rejoiced that they had such loving people. This scene of adoration lasted a very long time.

It was as more gifts were being brought to them that one of the spike-covered spheres moved. Up until that time, they had stayed motionless. Now, one rolled towards Daniel and Ruth. The first tree saw what was happening and shouted at the sphere to stop. It ignored the first tree's demand to stop and rolled right up to Daniel and Ruth. Its thorns pierced their legs. The pain that they both felt was intense and they cried out. They looked at the sphere. It changed into the shape of a glass person.

'I'm so sorry', it said to Ruth and Daniel, 'We are trapped. We gave in to temptation and nothing can be done. But we can help you. Go!'

The first tree appeared over the sphere that had become a glass person.

'You stupid thing!', the tree said and stamped on it.

Everything changed. When the pain subsided they looked up and all of the people that had been adoring them disintegrated into dust and the food and wine they had been eating was, in reality, rotting. They felt sick and realised that all they had experienced was an illusion. A trick.

'Why have you done this to us?', said Ruth, 'We are the Glassmaker's children!'

The first tree grew larger, shook violently and exploded into dust.

Daniel and Ruth held onto each other and felt themselves spinning faster and faster.

Chapter 20 - Jonah discovers a terrible truth

Jonah was freezing in the cell. An icy wind had arisen and his cell was open to the elements that blew against the walls of the Shattered Lord's castle. He looked around but could see nothing but the inside of his cell and the outside view of the world that his cell afforded. He could see no other cells or prisoners. But he could hear them. He heard the crying and the wailing. The shouting and the screaming, as hundreds of glass people who had been taken prisoner, waited for their uncertain and frightening future. He tried not to think about his future as it made his heart skip a beat in fear. Then his thoughts wandered to Daniel and Ruth. What had happened to them? Where were they? Were they still alive or had the Glassmaker indeed melted them down for His own means?

As he was wondering about them he heard the door of his cell rattle and then open. Two grey soldiers entered his cell and ordered him to follow them. When he hesitated for a moment they both grabbed him roughly and half dragged him out of the cell.

'What's happening? Where are you taking me?', he cried out, but the soldiers ignored him.

They descended to the ground floor of the castle and Jonah recognised the room with the orange glow. Many glass people were being directed to enter the room between lines of grey soldiers. The two soldiers escorting Jonah took him past the line of glass people and straight through the door.

In that room was a horror that so vile that Jonah felt as though he would be sick and all strength left his body.

He saw the line of glass people being guided toward a furnace, on top of which was a large, bubbling walkway. The people offered no resistance. It was as though they had lost all hope. The soldiers, who wore protective clothing against the heat of the furnace, steered the people into the furnace and to their death. Those glass people who became aware of what was happening at the last minute were roughly pushed by the guards onto the glowing walkway. As they walked onto the walkway, screams emerged from their mouths as they melted into a liquid and were no more. The bubbling liquid was then drained into a large vat, where it was kept until it was needed.

Jonah realised that he was going to be melted.

Chapter 21 - Jonah meets the shattered lord

Jonah's heart beat so fast that he thought he would explode with fear. The soldiers led him closer and closer to the bubbling walkway over the furnace and he could feel his body getting hotter and hotter and starting to liquify.

He struggled and tried to get free of the soldiers, but they were too strong. He closed his eyes and stopped fighting them, waiting for the inevitable.

Then, he felt himself being dragged away from the furnace, the soldiers laughing at him.

He overheard them say, 'Now he will bow to the Shattered Lord. All that resistance has been purified by the fire'.

The stress was too much for him and he fainted.

He came around as he was thrown onto the floor in a large dark room. It took a few minutes for his eyes to adjust to the darkness. Slowly he could make out the forms of guards around the edge of the large room and eventually his eyes rested on an almighty throne moulded out of melted glass. It looked deformed and bulbous and on it sat the Shattered Lord.

Jonah screamed and tried to back away from him, but soldiers prevented him.

The Shattered Lord was grotesque and misshapen. He looked like a million shards of discoloured glass held together by something.

The Shattered Lord stood up and as he stood up, it sounded like fingernails being scratched across a chalkboard. He walked across to Jonah and put his ugly, deformed face right up to Jonah's. Jonah turned his face away, but it didn't do any good.

The Shattered Lord put one of his fingers on the cheek of Jonah and drew it down, scratching and fracturing Jonah's cheek.

Jonah cried out in pain, but the Shattered Lord kept scratching him.

Eventually, he stopped.

The Shattered Lord spoke in a scratchy, painful voice.

'I have to commend you', he said to Jonah, 'You ran away from the Glassmaker. That shows good judgement. You came to me. That shows even better judgement.'

Jonah didn't see any point in saying that he hadn't come to the castle by his own choice but was forced.

'The Glassmaker is not all good. In fact, He causes pain. He melts people down', continued the Shattered Lord. He omitted the fact that the Glassmaker melted people in order to reform them into who they were meant to be, without fractures, but Jonah didn't know that.

Jonah spoke up, even though he was terrified.

'But, you melt people down also. I've seen it. I've felt it', he said.

'Yes, I do. How else will I fix the cracks in me?' he replied.

With those words, a large vat was brought into the throne room. The Shattered Lord dipped his hand into the boiling, bubbling liquid and started to repair the cracks in his body.

The Shattered Lord was repairing the fractures on his body with the melted remains of the glass people.

Chapter 22 - The shattered lord tells Jonah what to do

Jonah recoiled in horror as he realised that the people he had seen melted in the furnace room, were now being used to fix and repair the Shattered Lord.

The Shattered Lord saw the look on Jonah's face and smiled.

'You think I am a monster?' he said to Jonah, 'But I am not the monster. I am your saviour. The Glassmaker is the monster. I served him and He betrayed me!'

Jonah gasped as he heard those words.

'You served the Glassmaker?' Jonah said quietly.

'Yes!', boomed the Shattered Lord, 'and for his betrayal, I will make him pay'.

'But, how are you our saviour? You are melting us!', said Jonah

'Yes, yes, yes', replied the Shattered Lord flippantly, 'Sacrifices have to be made. But who else will protect you against the Glassmaker? Anyway, I am not here to debate with you. I am here to order you to do my work.'

'I don't want to do your work', whimpered Jonah

'You don't have a choice', said the Shattered Lord, and with a movement of his hand, a screen appeared showing the cells on the walls of the castle. The image zoomed into one cell in particular.

Jonah recognised his family.

'No!', he cried out tears flowing down his scratched face.

The Shattered Lord laughed.

'Yes. Isn't it lovely how I bring families together', he said, 'I need you to fight Daniel and Ruth. When they see you they will hesitate and at that moment I will strike them down'.

'They're alive?', cried out Jonah, 'Why hurt them!'

'Yes, they are alive. I can foresee that Daniel and Ruth will cause problems for me. They think that they know who they are and they think that they walk in the authority of the Glassmaker. That can cause problems for me and I want them out of the way' responded the Shattered Lord.

'No, I won't do that', said Jonah defiantly.

The Shattered Lord moved to Jonah and struck him across the face.

'Oh, I think you will', he sneered.

Chapter 23 - Out of the desert

Daniel and Ruth felt as though they would pass out from the spinning in the nowhere desert. They were not sure what was going to happen next. They had survived three tests. How many more were there going to be?

The whiteness of the nowhere desert started to change slowly. It started to go brown and then green and then blue. Just when they felt that they could take no more, Daniel and Ruth were spat out of the desert and both landed with a crash on the ground.

They looked at the desert they had just left. Was that the end of the testing or was this part of the trial? They waited in silence, looking at each other and then back to the desert.

Suddenly, they saw the desert contort and they braced themselves for another testing. The desert twisted and warped. There was a loud spitting noise and Noah was unceremoniously ejected from the desert. He landed with a thud and looked at Daniel and Ruth. Jade, Ranger and Firestone were thrown from the desert, as though the desert was disgusted with them all.

They landed in a crumpled heap on top of one another.

'Get off me', yelled Firestone and pushed Ranger away.

Ranger landed on his back. Instead of getting cross, he started to laugh. Jade joined in and then Noah. They looked at Daniel and Ruth who, by this time, were also laughing. Perhaps, it was just the relief of getting through the testing. Maybe, it was because everyone survived the desert. They were rolling around the ground in fits of laughter when Ruth spoke.

'Everyone quiet', she said.

No one listened. They kept on laughing.

'EVERYONE QUIET', she shouted.

At this, everyone did stop laughing.

'What's wrong?', said Daniel, 'Can't we just be happy for a moment!'

He saw that Ruth was gazing at something. Noah, Jade, Ranger and Firestone also saw that Ruth was focused on something nearby.

They followed her gaze.

Nearby, standing up, with swords drawn, was a detachment of grey soldiers. They had been waiting for anyone who had made it through the desert.

Chapter 24 - The chase to the forest

'RUN!', shouted Noah.

He need not have said this, as the troop of shining ones were already up and running. They were vastly outnumbered.

At first, they were running in random directions, just trying to keep out of reach of the grey soldiers. However, they couldn't do that forever.

"Look, over there,' shouted Ranger to the others, 'Get to the forest'.

The shining ones didn't need to be asked again. In unison, they all started to head for the forest. At least in the forest, they could hide. It wasn't a great plan, but it was a plan.

In the throne room of the Shattered Lord, Jonah and the lord were watching the chase on a large fractured glass screen. The Shattered Lord was laughing, as he saw that the grey soldiers were gaining on the shining ones. He was confident that his soldiers would catch them before they entered the forest. Jonah was secretly willing his friends to run faster, tears running down his cheeks. Whilst all this was happening, glass people were being melted to repair the Shattered Lord's brokenness.

'Run faster,' yelled Noah, aware that the grey soldiers were now very close to them all. He drew his sword and lashed out at a soldier who was just about to grab hold of him. The grey soldier stumbled and fell, tripping up several other grey soldiers. There were just too many of them to be beaten.

The shining ones were starting to lose hope of escape.

'Keep on running' shouted Daniel, 'DO NOT GIVE UP!'

'Over there,' said Firestone pointing to an opening in the dense forest.

Just as they were about to be overwhelmed, the band of shining ones ran through the opening in the forest. The forest opening immediately closed up, preventing the grey soldiers from entering.

The shining ones stopped running and looked back to where the opening had been. It was completely sealed off. No one could get through. They breathed a sigh of relief.

However, their relief was short lived. The forest was dark and oppressive. Strange noises echoed through the forest of pine trees. The low hanging branches grasped at their heads and shoulders as if the trees were trying to take them prisoner.

That was when the ground began to move.

Chapter 25 - Beginnings 6

The doors of the Glassmaker's chamber flew open and spirit beings burst into the room to see what was happening, only to come to a sudden stop when they saw the glory of the Glassmaker and the small grey figure of Ramiel. He was barely recognisable and looked so fragile. Tabbris stood in front of him, as though to shield him from the Glassmaker.

To Tabbris and the others, who had just flooded into the room, it did look as though the Glassmaker was punishing Ramiel, which was not the case.

Those who had rushed into the room now reversed their route as they saw the Glassmaker continue to grow in authority and splendour. It was a terrifying and wonderful sight.

The Glassmaker was not angry. He wasn't showing his glory to frighten those He had created. He wanted to show them that there was more to all they could see. There was more to what they knew and understood.

Tabbris remained in front of Ramiel.

'Stop it!', he cried out to the Glassmaker, 'Stop hurting him!'

The Glassmaker continued to shine his glory.

They thought it was thunder at first, but realised that it is just the Glassmaker talking.

'Will you bow the knee?', He said in a voice that shook the foundations of where they were all standing.

'Ramiel, will you bow the knee?', the Glassmaker repeated.

All those who had gathered looked at Ramiel. Many could see that it was not the Glassmaker who was hurting him, but it was Ramiel who was hurting himself. Some though, only saw Ramiel in pain and being distorted and blamed the Glassmaker.

The voice reverberated for several minutes, the ground shaking. Ramiel eventually turned to face the Glassmaker, even though the glory of the Glassmaker caused pain in his eyes and body. He felt as though he was being burnt alive.

He defiantly stood as tall as he could and with a gravelly voice he replied with a rebellious, 'No!'

Chapter 26 - Beginnings 7

At that second, every spirit being in the Glassmaker's kingdom knew the power of a single moment. They faced a choice and they had to act on that choice immediately, for at that moment two armies appeared. Those who were for the Glassmaker and those who were for Ramiel. Those who were for Ramiel weren't exactly against the Glassmaker. They were for Ramiel because they thought it was the Glassmaker who was harming him. They were also unbalanced by the creation of the glass people and the glass world. Like Ramiel they believed that they were being sidelined in favour of the glass people. So, they opposed the Glassmaker. The power of a single moment created two opposing armies and brokenness spread.

Light and dark clashed for the first time. Friends against friends. Division and hurt. Sparks flew as swords were drawn. One moment they were on the same side, as there had only been one side - the Glassmakers. Now those who had laughed together and worshipped together, now battled against each other trying to get the upper hand. Those supporting Ramiel becoming increasingly sure that they were in the right. Those supporting the Glassmaker fighting for his honour.

It looked as though the majority of the spirit beings had

sided with Ramiel and that those loyal to the Glassmaker were vastly outnumbered. It had looked as though the darkness would overcome the light.

Then, one word shook every spirit being to their core and immobilised every living thing.

'STOP!', declared the Glassmaker.

What was declared happened. Everyone was motionless. Those on the side of Ramiel now grey and fractured. Those in the Glassmaker's army standing firm and shining.

The Glassmaker changed into the form that He usually took and walked up to Ramiel. Tears were in the Glassmaker's eyes, and then He declared another word to Ramiel and all who had sided with him.

'Go!'

Chapter 27 - Pine Cone Forest

Daniel, Ruth, Noah, Jade, Ranger and Firestone started to panic. There was nowhere for them to go. The tree trunks had no low hanging branches upon which they could all climb to safety. They hopped around the ground trying to get rid of the pine cones that were starting to cling to their bodies.

They all looked at each other, and then looked around for a means of escape. None could be seen. They only saw what looked like large piles of pine cones dotted over the forest. As they looked at the pine cones climbing upon their bodies and then back at the large piles of pine cones, they realised, with horror, that the large piles of pine cones were actually shining ones who had been trapped.

They panicked all the more, struggling to brush the encroaching pine cones.

'Why are they doing this? Why are they covering us?', cried out Ranger.

'There is strange magic happening here and it is not good', said Firestone.

'It's because we are going towards the Shattered Lord and away from the Glassmaker', shouted Ruth.

The pine cones didn't give up. No matter how many they brushed off, many more continued to climb onto them.

Eventually, all of them were covered up to their necks and unable to move.

'Never give up', said Daniel.

Then all was quiet, as everyone was imprisoned by the pine cones. They were like statues.

It was hard not to feel hopeless. It felt like the end of the journey.

Inside his pine cone cocoon, Daniel felt despondent. He heard something move around him. Not just one thing, but many things.

'Help!', he yelled.

Something climbed up his body and he felt as though this was the end as he realised that the moving things might not want to help them, but destroy them. His heart was beating faster and fear was rising not just in him, but in all his friends.

There was movement on his face. Something pulled the pine cones on his face and eventually, a pine cone covering his eye was pried away.

With one eye Daniel was staring into the eyes of a chimpanzee.

Chapter 28 - Beginnings 8

It wasn't a request, but a command to be followed, and Ramiel and those who followed him could not resist and they felt themselves fall out of the presence of the Glassmaker and into darkness. Fear took hold of them all as they felt alone for the first time. As they fell away from the light they fractured and distorted and began to live in the darkness. The fear fuelled anger within them and for aeons they fought with each other in the darkness, Ramiel destructively ruling over them. He had his wish - he was a ruler now. Only his kingdom was not one of love, but of fear and brokenness. They were all broken - not just in their spirit bodies, but in their hearts. Some became so consumed with rage that when they fought with others they transfigured into beasts made up of shards of glass. Not recognisable as the once beautiful spirit beings they had been.

Ramiel never forgot about the Glassmaker and continually thought of ways to hurt Him. But they couldn't reach him. Every time they tried to approach his realm the light was too strong and they started to melt and had to retreat.

A cry had come out from Tabbris who was now as deformed and broken as Ramiel.

'Look', he shouted, 'Over there!'.

Ramiel and his fractured army looked to where Tabbris

was pointing.

It was the glass world, with all the glass people, that the Glassmaker had created. Shiny bright. Unbroken. Unaware of the descending legion of pain that was coming towards it.

'There is my revenge', sneered Ramiel

They all descended to the glass world and broke it.

Chapter 29 - The animals awaken the shining ones

Daniel recognised the chimpanzee from the garden, from before they entered the Glassmaker's House. The animals had helped them in the garden and now they were helping them in the forest.

Albert the chimpanzee smiled.

'I can't pull the pine cones off you. They are too strong in their attachment. They are attracted to fear', he said to Daniel.

'What can we do?' Daniel replied in a muffled voice.

'Believe', responded Albert.

Then he said these words to Daniel: The Glassmaker is coming.

As Daniel listened to the words, he felt hope rise within him. He had struggled so much in going through the battles of the desert, escaping the soldiers and getting trapped in the forest, that he had forgotten about the Glassmaker.

The words Albert spoke awakened within him the memory of the goodness of the Glassmaker. As the awakening increased, so the fear decreased. One by one, the pine cones started to fall away from him. Soon his face was uncovered and he could see all of the other animals going from each trapped shining one, uttering the words, 'The Glassmaker is coming' and awakening faith within each person.

Soon, all of the shining ones were free, some of whom had been kept prisoner by the pine cones for a very long time.

Daniel and Ruth embraced each other and looked into each other's eyes. The moment was broken when laughter echoed through the forest.

Chapter 30 - The hermit of the forest speaks

Fleck, the large wolf, growled at the laughter, the glass heckles on its back standing up.

To the surprise of everyone, Oswald the owl flew down from one of the trees where he had been observing everything and landed on the ground.

'It's okay Fleck', he said, 'This is a friend, not a foe'.

With those words, a presence emerged out of the forest. The figure was so bright that they all had to shield their eyes from the light. They couldn't make out a form, they only felt something powerful, yet they didn't feel afraid.

The light made the shadows of the pine trees dance, as it made its way to where they were all standing. The sight reminded Daniel and Ruth when they were visited in the forest by Nathaniel, the first shining one they had met. The light came right up to Daniel and Ruth and stopped. Just when they felt that the light would damage their eyes, it started to reduce in intensity and slowly a figure appeared and before them, stood a very old man with a smiling face.

Oswald spoke first to the old man, 'You are the Hermit of the Forest.'

The hermit looked at Oswald and smiled.

'Yes I am', he replied.

There was a ripple of voices as the shining ones spoke to

each other in amazement.

'The who?', asked Daniel.

'I am the hermit and I have been waiting for a very long time for this moment. My Lord, the Glassmaker, spoke to me and told me that this was the time', said the hermit.

'The time for what?', asked Ruth.

The hermit was silent for a moment as he looked around all of the shining ones and all of the animals.

'The time for everything to be put right', he replied, 'The Glassmaker is coming, and Daniel and Ruth - He wants you to lead the army'.

Chapter 31 - How to confuse the flying monsters

The soldiers had expected one of the larger and older warriors to be chosen. But that was not the plan of the Glassmaker. He wanted to choose a leader, or leaders, who would not rely on their own experience but would rely on the Glassmaker.

'Everyone looked at Daniel and Ruth.

Daniel and Ruth laughed, and then stopped abruptly as they realised that the hermit was not joking.

Then questions came tumbling out of them both.

'Why us?'

'Why not use someone with more experience?'

'We don't know how to lead an army!'

'Send someone else!'

The hermit just stood silently and let them speak.

It was Albert, the chimpanzee, who stopped them.

'Excuse me. Why not let the hermit speak?', he said bashfully.

Daniel and Ruth stopped questioning, looked at Albert and then at the hermit.

'Sorry', said Daniel

The hermit smiled and continued.

'I know you have many questions and there are many here who could lead the army. However, the Glassmaker has chosen you', he said.

'But we don't know how', replied Ruth

'Trust him', answered the hermit.

He continued, 'All of you here love the Glassmaker. You are here because you want to see the Glass Kingdom healed and restored. You want to see Ramiel, the Shattered Lord, defeated. You want the Glassmaker's Kingdom here. Follow His leading. Follow Daniel and Ruth.'

One by one the shining ones moved to stand behind Daniel and Ruth in a sign that they would follow them. Daniel and Ruth looked at the soldiers and then at each other and then at the hermit.

They nodded to him in a sign that they would do what they had been asked to do.

'There is the little problem of getting past the flying monsters', said Oswald, 'We have no idea of how to do that'.

Everyone nodded in agreement.

'There is only one way to get past', said the hermit, ' Sing in praise of the Glassmaker. The song will confuse the enemy!'

Chapter 32 - Jonah is terrified

The Shattered Lord's throne room was a dark, grey, depressing room. There was no joy or light in it and as soon as you walked into it you became aware of the oppressive atmosphere. A cracked glass throne stood at the end and on it the Shattered Lord sat, smiling and assured that all would go his way.

He saw that Jonah was looking at the fragile glass throne on which he sat.

'Beautiful isn't it', he said

Jonah remained silent.

At that moment, a grey messenger came into the room.

'What is it?', said the lord gruffly.

The messenger looked at Jonah.

The Shattered Lord stood up and went over to the messenger. He grabbed his cheeks and forced the messenger to look into his eyes.

'Look at me, not him, and tell me your message is!', he shouted.

'The shining ones in pine cone forest have been freed and they have spoken to the hermit', mumbled the messenger.

The Shattered Lord threw him backwards onto the ground and the messenger raced out of the room glad to escape.

The Shattered Lord growled and tensed. More fractures

appeared over his body.

Jonah stood silently looking at him and then at his throne, appalled at how it had been made.

The Shattered Lord noticed Jonah looking at his throne

'Do you want to know how many people were melted down to make this throne?', continued the lord, smirking as he saw the horror that came across Jonah's face.

Chapter 33 - Jonah has no option, but to obey

Jonah wanted to be back in his cell. A strange desire, but he felt so unsafe in the presence of the Shattered Lord as if anything could and would happen. He felt his prison cell would be safer than in the throne room.

Another messenger entered the room and whispered to his lord. A smile came across the lord's face, and he looked at Jonah.

'Bring them in', he said

Jonah felt a sense of dread.

He was right to feel it. He watched in horror as he saw his family escorted into the room. His mother. His father. His brother. He barely recognised them, broken and dirty as they were. They hung their heads in despair, staring at the floor, as they were roughly pushed into the room.

'No! Don't', cried out Jonah and he started to run to them. Not only did a soldier stop him, but his family recoiled at the sight of a grey person running at them.

Jonah realised that they didn't recognise him and he wept.

'It's me, Jonah', he said to them, 'Don't you recognise me?'

His family stared at him. They didn't recognise the face, but they recognised the voice.

'Jonah?', his mother cried out, 'You're alive! What have they done to you? Why are you grey like the soldiers?'

Through a fog of tears and joy, Jonah's family called out to him.

'So touching', said the Shattered Lord sarcastically.

The family became aware of the Shattered Lord for the first time and tried to get away from him, but they were stopped by the grey soldiers.

He went and stood beside Jonah and in a calculated act, he put his arm around Jonah and smiled.

Jonah flinched and tried to get away, but the Shattered Lord held him firmly.

His family were so confused by this. What was happening?

Eventually, it was his father who spoke.

'It was you', he said to Jonah, 'You betrayed us. Look at yourself. You are grey, like all the other soldiers. You have joined the enemy's army!'

Jonah started to deny all this and tell his father that he was so mistaken, but the Shattered Lord stopped him.

'Take that vermin out of this room and let me talk to my friend', he said, looking at Jonah.

Chapter 34 - Jonah's family thinks he has betrayed them

The last words that Jonah heard his father shout was 'you betrayed us…'.

Jonah was numb from all that was happening. All because he had made the choice not to stay with the Glassmaker. All because he thought he knew best. All because he would not trust. He was broken outside and inside.

'You can save your family', said the Shattered Lord quietly, 'And in the future, they may be able to find out the truth that you did not betray them.'

Jonah was cornered and he knew it.

'You face a difficult choice. You can let your family think you betrayed them and save Daniel and Ruth. Or you can betray Daniel and Ruth and save your family from being melted down and becoming part of the furniture in my throne room!'

Jonah's mind was in turmoil. As he closed his eyes he saw himself with Daniel and Ruth laughing and running away from Constable Bunce. He watched, in his mind, as he and his friends had overcome the obstacles that faced them on the journey to the Glassmaker's house. He remembered how they had to work together to overcome and finish the journey.

Then he remembered the reason for the journey. His family.

'What is it you want me to do? he asked

'I want you to distract Daniel and Ruth long enough in order for me to capture them and melt them down', came the reply, 'When they see you they will hesitate and that will be enough opportunity to trap them'.

Jonah was the one who felt trapped. He knew that he couldn't trust the Shattered Lord, but he couldn't refuse the possibility of saving his family.

He sighed, looked at the Shattered Lord and said, with deep regret, 'I'll do it'.

Chapter 35 - A growing army

All of the shining ones and animals tensed as cracking noises arose from within the forest. It was like someone breaking a stick over their knee, only louder. They all looked around and drew out their swords. The hermit, who had lived in the forest for hundreds of years, stood calmly watching everyone.

'What is that noise?' called out Albert.

The cracking continued all around them. Suddenly, the trees near them started to writhe in the ground and shake as though they were being uprooted.

Oswald flew up, searching for a reason for the cracking noise.

Looking down, he could see things emerging from the roots of the trees.

'Watch out,' he shouted, 'there are things coming from the roots of the trees!'

All of the shining ones and animals turned to face the tree that was nearest to them and, sure enough, something was emerging from the roots of many of the trees.

Everyone was ready to attack whatever vile creatures exited the roots.

At this point, the hermit spoke.

'What is coming out of the ground does not need your anger, but your help,' he said.

They looked at the hermit and then back to the twisting roots, confused at what was happening.

'I see a face,' yelled one of the soldiers.

'So do I,' said another, voices echoing throughout the forest.

One by one the trees gave up their prisoners and it was not vile creatures that were revealed, but more shining ones!

'What is this?' said Noah, running over to help one of the trapped people out of their horrible grave.

Those who were released from the tree roots were dazed and confused, but very quickly they stood up and gained strength.

'Who are these people?' Daniel asked the hermit.

'They are the ones who fell asleep. Like you, they had gone through the desert and were on a mission for the Glassmaker, but tiredness tempted them to sleep in the forest. Whilst they were sleeping they were taken prisoner by the roots of the trees. Now they are free,' answered the hermit simply.

'But why have they been released now?' asked Ruth.

The hermit looked at the growing army of shining ones and animals and said, 'They were released because the Glassmaker is coming and He is awakening His army.'

Chapter 36 - Daniel and Ruth lead the army

There was a large number of people and animals standing in the forest. A growing army of people and animals.

Daniel and Ruth were still standing beside the hermit, watching all that was happening and waiting for someone to tell them how to lead.

Some of the shining ones had been trapped for many years, some nearly as old as the hermit. They greeted one another and the hermit and mixed with those who had been trapped by the pine cones. Laughter arose and the forest didn't seem threatening anymore. It seemed brighter than before.

Daniel and Ruth could hear parts of different conversations.

'I've been trapped for 200 years,' said one person who started to look younger and younger the longer he was free.

'What was it like in the tree roots?' asked one who had been held captive by the pine cone

'It was like a bad dream, but you are awake,' answered one.

'It was as though you were trying to run away from a danger you couldn't see, but you were unable to run,' replied another.

And so, the conversations made connections and connections became the building blocks for future friendships.

The hermit was smiling at all that was happening. He had been here from the beginning and his role was to prepare for the coming of the Glassmaker. He recognised that his job was almost completed and that made him glad. After a while, his countenance changed and he called out, 'Quiet!'

The hermit was not aggressive when he spoke, but it was a firm command and soon all the voices in the forest were silent.

Everyone looked at the hermit.

'My job here is almost done,' he said, 'I have been preparing for the coming of the Glassmaker and He is nearly here.'

Excited voices rose at this news.

The hermit continued, 'But there is still work to be done before He does. There are still sacrifices to be made and some of you have a bigger mission than you realise.'

As he said this, the hermit looked at Daniel and Ruth.

They smiled nervously.

'What does he mean,' whispered Ruth to Daniel.

'Haven't a clue,' he replied

'You are part of the Glassmaker's army. You may not feel like it or look like it at this moment, but that is who you are,' said the hermit, 'Daniel and Ruth have been chosen to lead. Follow well. Fight courageously. Have faith. You are the Glassmaker's children.'

All of the soldiers and animals shouted and sang out the Glassmaker's name.

Chapter 37 - Preparing to get past the flying monsters

Daniel and Ruth continued to make every kind of excuse as to why they were not the people to lead the army. They insisted that there were other hardened warriors far more qualified to lead than they were, but every objection they put up was answered by this one phrase: 'The Glassmaker has chosen you so we will follow.'

Eventually, Daniel and Ruth had to accept that they were the leaders of this army and that the Glassmaker had chosen them, even though they did not feel qualified.

Noah walked up to them and smiled. There was no jealousy in his face even though he had been the senior soldier in the company that Daniel and Ruth had joined.

'So, what are your orders?' he asked them.

Jade, Ranger and Firestorm had joined them.

'What do you think we should do?' asked Ruth, 'We feel honoured, but we are completely out of our depth. We need your help.'

'Of course, we will help,' said Noah.

He continued, 'There is a large number of flying monsters that surrounds the Shattered Lord's Castle and the prison where the families are being held.'

'Yes, hundreds of them. Huge and nasty,' added in Firestone.

'We will create a break in the barrier and the majority of the army can get through,' said Noah.

'What do you mean the majority of the army? Surely you mean the whole army?' asked Ruth nervously.

The troop looked at each other, not wanting to go on. Oswald had flown down beside them and said what they did not want to say.

'Some will not make it past the flying monsters. There will need to be a large group of volunteers who will sing the battle-song. In singing the song, they will become the target of the flying monsters and grey soldiers. Many will not make it,' said Oswald.

'No!' cried out Daniel and Ruth simultaneously.

'There is no other way,' said Ranger.

'And we volunteer to lead the battle-song,' added Firestone.

Chapter 38 - The day the plan unfolds

The Shattered Lord's castle and stronghold was in the centre of a huge crater. High hills surrounded the castle. At the foot of the hills was a wall of flying monsters and grey soldiers, encircling the castle and the prison, which was called Gehenna.

The Glassmaker's army, or at least the part of the army that was now led by Daniel and Ruth, stood at the top of the high hills, looking down at the wall of monsters and at the seemingly impregnable fortress.

Their hearts were beating fast at the task they faced. They looked at the prison cells built on the wall of the castle and wondered where their families were and if they were still alive. The thought of their families being safe filled them with strength. As they stood facing the impossible task, they both became aware of a gentle presence, as though the wind was blowing in their faces, even though the air was completely still. They closed their eyes and heard the words, 'I am with you'.

'The Glassmaker,' breathed out Ruth.

Daniel and Ruth looked at each other.

Daniel shouted, 'Let the battle-song begin!'

The flying monsters, even though they had bad eyesight and couldn't see what was happening, were restless. They could sense something was about to happen. The grey soldiers became agitated because the flying monsters, or splinter cats, were pulling at the restraints that held them down.

Ranger and Firestone stepped out in front of a large group of shining ones. They had all volunteered for this job, knowing that it could be their last act. They all closed their eyes and raised their hands and they began to sing.

The harmonies were so beautiful it made you cry. The words were so moving that you wanted to bow down and worship the Glassmaker.

'You have made us and we are yours,' they sang in honour of the Glassmaker, 'and we surrender all to you. Glory, glory, glory!'

The group of singers started to glow brighter and brighter. Firestone began to glow a fiery red. The splinter cats howled in pain at the beautiful song. Several broke free of their restraints and flew around confused and in pain. The soldiers struggled to control them, but a few managed to get onto their monsters and mobilise them towards the singers. They headed directly for them. The first monsters to arrive seemed to do nothing, but as more and more of the splinter cats arrived the song became stronger, as one by one the singers were bombarded by shards of glass from the tails of the splinter cats and by the swords of the grey soldiers. The song grew louder and the shining ones became brighter. When the song became almost too beautiful to listen to, an explosion of light enveloped all the surrounding hills. The splinter cats were thrown across the hills by the explosion. Some simply disintegrated.

As this was happening, gaps appeared in the wall of splinter cats, and the rest of the Glassmaker's army ran down the hills, through the gaps the singing and subsequent explosion had created, attacking any stray monsters or soldiers.

Daniel and Ruth made it through the wall and when they were a safe distance behind the remaining wall of splinter cats, they looked back at where the singers had been. Not one shining one was left.

Noah stood beside them, weeping.

'Firestone and Ranger, one day we shall meet again', he said and then turned to face the unholy stronghold.

Chapter 39 - Hope starts to rise in Gehenna

The cells of the fortress were built on the outside, giving the occupants a prime view of the hills. When the song started, hope began to rise within the hearts of those in prison. The prison had a name - Gehenna. In some forgotten language it meant rubbish dump.

The condition of the cells was disgusting and those held within were kept alive by the most basic of foods. However, nothing starts to kindle life than the recognition that freedom might be coming. People can feed themselves with the hope that is like the best of foods.

Some in the cells could see that the splinter cats were becoming restless.

'Look!' cried out one, pointing to the hills.

Those who were able to move quickly ran to the bars of their prison and looked up to the hills. They saw the Glassmaker's army and then they saw the singers shine. They saw the confusion and the noise and the fighting. They saw the army run down the hill towards them and the possibility of rescue entered their thoughts. Could it be possible that they would escape this horrible place?

Sarah, Daniel's sister, reached the bars of her cell before her parents Peter and Martha. They were both weak from lack of food and the cold wind that blew in through the open face of the prison. Constable Bunce sat in the corner.

'What's happening?' he asked 'What can you see? Who is singing?'

'I can see freedom', replied Peter, Daniel's father.

Chapter 40 - Gehenna - the prison of the Shattered Lord

Ramiel was watching what was happening on the fractured glass screen in his throne room. His officers were nervously looking around wondering what he was going to do. It was Tabbris, his aide from when they had served the Glassmaker, who spoke first. Tabbris, like all of those who had followed Ramiel, was disfigured and broken beyond recognition. Once beautiful, he now looked horrific.

'What should we do?' he asked

No reply came.

'What should we do?' he repeated, and this time Ramiel snarled at his former aide.

Eventually, Ramiel spoke.

'This is not the whole of the Glassmaker's army, only part of it. This time they are not here to defeat us, they are here to rescue the prisoners. Drop the screens on all of the cells in Gehenna,' he said.

'What good will that do?' asked Tabbris bravely.

Ramiel turned sharply and walked up to Tabbris, pressing his face right up to the face of Tabbris.

'When the cells were open, the prisoners felt vulnerable, open to attack. Now they can see an army coming towards them they need to make them blind so that fear starts to rise up within them. It will also make it more difficult for the invaders to find the prisoners. Now do it!' shouted Ramiel.

Immediately, everyone left the throne room to follow their lord's commands.

'Tabbris,' called Ramiel, 'don't ever question me again! Now go and double the guard on the gates. There is going to be a fight.'

Chapter 41 - The gates of Gehenna

The gates of Gehenna were not what they had been expecting. They hadn't really thought about gates being a big deal. They imagined they would just barge through and fight. As soon as they saw the gates they realised that it would not be so easy.

The gates were huge broken mirrors. As the army ran up to the gates, they witnessed their reflection in the gates. They tried to force the gates open. They tried to break the gates. They tried to climb the gates. Nothing would open the gates or bring them down.

'This is so frustrating!' said Jade, kicking the gates once more, 'We are so close.'

Albert tried to climb the gates, but there was nothing to grab hold onto in order to climb up.

There was a growing uneasiness among the troops. The splinter cats and grey soldiers were regrouping and preparing to chase the Glassmaker's army. The army had nowhere to go. At that moment they were trapped.

It was Ruth who spoke up.

'Do you remember when Michael gave us our orders just after we had been made new?' she said to Daniel

'Yes,' he replied, but not really understanding.

Ruth continued, 'He said, "When you can't go forward,

kneel and ask for help." Well, we can't go forward and we are going to be attacked from behind, so I say kneel.'

Daniel looked around trying to see if there was any other option.

Ruth didn't wait for him to agree. She knelt on the ground and one by one the Glassmaker's army knelt. It was a strange sight. An apparently impregnable wall in front of them and an angry army amassing behind them. It didn't seem the sensible thing to do, but obedience often doesn't look sensible.

'Glassmaker, we can't see a way forward so we look to you to help us,' said Ruth. She felt strange saying the words. She wasn't even sure what she was doing.

At first, nothing happened. Then, a breeze blew over them, much like the one they had felt at the top of the hills. But this wind grew in strength. It became ferocious and the gates of Gehenna started to rattle as they were shaken back and forth. Ruth, Daniel and the army continued kneeling, hearts beating fast, some holding onto each other so that they would not be blown away.

The gates shook violently as the wind persisted in battering the stronghold. They heard a horrific crack and the gates fell down under the power of the wind.

The Glassmaker's soldiers were still kneeling, but all looked up to see the enemy soldiers with their swords drawn.

Chapter 42 - The battle in Gehenna

The grey soldiers were confused and in disarray, but they were dangerous and not afraid. They stood aggressively and ready for battle.

Daniel and Ruth stood, as did the rest of the army. They felt a courage rise within them that was beyond who they were. Daniel who was always afraid of getting into trouble now ran at the trouble, Ruth running by his side. The rest of their army followed and the two rival groups met at the entrance where the gates of Gehenna now lay shattered on the ground.

Swords clashed and the shining ones looked glorious as they flew into battle. They were shining brighter than ever before and the grey soldiers were blinded by the light.

Noah and Jade were roaring as they fought one enemy after another.

Noah shouted at Daniel and Ruth, whilst fighting with two grey soldiers.

'Go and release the prisoners. That's what Michael ordered us to do,' he yelled, 'and find your families. Take them through the furnace room. There is a back exit. It will be safer.'

Daniel and Ruth nodded, knowing it would be useless to argue, and ran towards the wall where the cells were embedded.

They were not sure where to go or how to find their families, but they noticed a door by the first cell where grey soldiers were standing guard watching the battle and ready for any intruders.

Daniel and Ruth charged at them and rather than standing their ground, the two soldiers guarding the door ran away.

Daniel and Ruth entered a room through the door and were attacked. Although Daniel and Ruth had never been taught how to fight, they found themselves using the swords rather well. They felt empowered by some unseen good that guided their hands. As soon as the blades of their swords touched the grey soldiers, the soldiers disintegrated, leaving Daniel and Ruth alone in the room.

They looked around the dark room which seemed to hold the keys for the cells. They looked at each other and took them from the hooks and went in the direction where they thought the cells were.

There were so many cells and so little time that Daniel and Ruth were unsure if setting everyone free would be possible, but they knew that their families were here somewhere. There was no option, but to try every door.

They started to unlock the doors closest to them and looked in. It was dark and cold. The brightness they carried lit up the room and the people imprisoned shaded their eyes from the glare. Their families were not in the cell.

'It's okay. We are here to help,' said Ruth, 'come and follow us.'

The people stood up and followed them.

They tried each door, and each time a group of people started to follow them. After a short time, many had been set free.

Daniel and Ruth wondered if their families were still alive and started to despair.

'Let's keep going,' said Daniel, and Ruth nodded.

They approached the last cells, with little hope, but a growing band of followers.

Ruth unlocked the door and stepped in.

Chapter 43 - The families in the cells

The families were in the dark. They could hear fighting and shouting but could see nothing. This made the darkness all the more terrifying. They all cowered in the corner of the cell, as far away from the door as possible. Daniel's family, along with Ruth's and Jonah's were in the same cell. It all seemed so long ago. The village of Knock seemed so far away.

The noise got closer and the families could hear clanging in the corridor outside.

'What's happening?' asked Martha.

'I'm scared,' cried Sarah, holding on tighter than ever to her mother and father.

However, no reply came. All eyes were fixed on the door. They could see a glowing light under the door. It got brighter until it was partially lighting up the cell. The door rattled and they heard the sound of a key being turned. Fear turned into noise as some started to weep and scream. They knew what happened to people in the cells, that they were taken and melted down to keep the Shattered Lord alive. They thought that their turn had come.

The door flew open and light flooded into the cell, extinguishing the darkness. Everyone in the cell shielded their eyes from the brightness.

'You are safe. Do not fear,' said a voice.

'We are here to save you,' said another.

Daniel and Ruth looked at the people in the cell and recognised their families. They ran up to their parents to embrace them, but their parents shrank back from them.

'Mother, father,' said Daniel, 'it's me, Daniel.'

His mother and father stopped moving and stared at this bright figure.

'It's true,' said Ruth to all in the room, 'we look different now. The Glassmaker has changed us, transformed us, healed us. But, it is still us.'

'Father,' said Daniel, 'the Glassmaker's furnace is real and it is a good thing!'

Nobody moved, apart from Martha. She stood up and tentatively walked to Daniel. She looked into his eyes and put her hand on his face. Her furrowed brow changed to a smile.

'It is you!' she cried out, 'it's my brother Daniel!'

Chapter 44 - Escaping by the furnace

Daniel's and Ruth's parents ran and embraced them, even though they didn't understand what was happening. It felt like a dream.

'Where is Jonah?' asked Joan, Jonah's mother.

Daniel and Ruth looked at each other and then at Joan.

Ruth gently took her hand in hers and looked into Joan's eyes.

'We don't know where he is. We got separated, but I am sure we will be able to find him', she said.

Tears streamed down Joan's face and her husband walked over and put his arm around her.

'We must all go now!', said Daniel

'But where should we go? How can we escape?' said Peter to his son.

'There is a way out but we must go past the Shattered Lord's furnace', replied Daniel.

People cried out in fear. They knew what happened in the furnace room.

'Don't be afraid. It is dangerous, but there is always hope. There is a way through this. Trust us', said Ruth.

Ruth's mother cupped Ruth's shining face in her hands.

'We do trust you. Lead the way', she said to Ruth.

Ruth smiled.

'Let's go', she said and walked through the crowd of glass people out of the cell.

She looked down the corridor and saw no-one.

'All the soldiers are outside fighting. Now is our only chance to get everyone out', she said to Daniel.

'Let's go', shouted Daniel and they all started to walk down the corridor to the stairs that led to the furnace room.

Everyone shuffled down the stairs and entered the furnace room. They were all scared, but the hope of freedom was stronger than their fear.

The furnace was glowing hot and the metal tray was still over the burning fire. There was a ledge that went around the edge of the furnace and at the end of the ledge a door that led to the outside and freedom.

'You don't want us to go over that ledge', asked Peter, 'it's too dangerous!'

'There is no other way father, we must go that way', replied Daniel.

Peter looked at his son and then at the ledge.

'Well, we should go now', he said

One by one the glass people moved along the narrow ledge, the furnace bubbling just below them. It was a slow process, but eventually, the last people made their way across. Just as they were doing so footsteps were heard in the hallway.

'Quickly!' said Daniel and encouraged the final people to go faster.

They kept their eyes on the entrance to the furnace room. Daniel and Ruth had started to go across when several grey soldiers entered the room and saw them.

'Get them!', shouted one and they started to head towards them.

Daniel and Ruth stopped moving, prepared to sacrifice themselves to let all the glass people escape. As they watched the grey soldiers approach, one drew their attention.

'Jonah?' said Ruth.

Chapter 45 - Daniel, Ruth and Jonah meet again

Daniel and Ruth didn't know whether to run towards Jonah because he was a friend and embrace him, or to run away from him because he was grey. So they all stood still looking at each other, whilst the glass people escaped. Jonah's parents were the last to leave and they had turned around when they heard Ruth speak Jonah's name.

'Jonah!' cried his mother, who tried to run towards her son, but was stopped by some of the glass people.

'Let me go!' his mother shouted as she struggled to escape, 'I want to be with my son!'

The soldiers with Jonah were eager to attack.

'Let's go and get them all!', shouted one soldier and they all started to move towards Daniel and Ruth.

Daniel and Ruth lifted their swords against the attackers and braced themselves for a fight.

'Run,' they shouted to those who were still in the furnace room.

Jonah's mother fought to get closer to her son, tears in her eyes.

Jonah stood still, confused by being confronted with his family and friends. His heart was being torn in two by the cries of his mother. He started to see that he had been wrong all along and that Daniel and Ruth had been right to trust the

Glassmaker. He needed to put right the wrongs he had done. But he was afraid. He looked up at his mother, struggling and weeping, and then at Daniel and Ruth. Pain and sorrow was etched on his face.

'Come with us,' called out Daniel.

The soldiers, who were advancing towards them stopped and turned to look at Jonah.

'You know them?' asked one.

After a moments pause, Jonah answered.

'Yes, I do,' he replied, 'and you will leave them alone!'

And with those words, he moved and stood facing the advancing grey soldiers, his sword drawn.

Chapter 46 - Jonah the hero

The grey soldiers looked at Jonah standing before them.

'You think you can stop us, you traitor!' said a soldier taking a step towards him.

Jonah took a step back. The soldier laughed at him.

Jonah's mind was in turmoil. His friends probably thought he was a traitor, and now these soldiers called him a traitor.

'I'm sorry', he called out to Daniel, Ruth and his family, ' I was scared and I thought I was doing the right thing. But I was wrong. I'm so sorry I left you. Tell my family that I didn't betray them.'

Tears ran down the faces of Daniel and Ruth.

'Come with us', implored Daniel.

'No', replied Jonah, 'I have to repair the damage that I have done. Run!'

And with that Jonah launched an attack on the grey soldiers.

'No!' cried Ruth and Daniel had to stop her from running to Jonah's side.

'We need to keep the people safe', cried Daniel to Ruth as she struggled in his arms.

Jonah fought bravely, with a strength that was not his own. He started to overpower the soldiers and one by one he drove them into the burning furnace. Eventually, there was only one left. They stood looking at each other, panting from the exertion of the fight.

Jonah took the initiative and brought his sword down upon the grey soldier. The soldier was caught off guard by the sudden attack and started to fall into the furnace. At the last moment, he reached up and grabbed Jonah by the arm, pulling him into the furnace.

Daniel, Ruth and Jonah's families cried out in despair as they watched Jonah fall, held by the soldier, into the fire. It all seemed to happen in slow motion and was too terrible to witness.

Daniel and Ruth thought they saw Jonah smile as he fell. All they could do was watch.

He landed in the flames and slowly melted until all you could see was his face. Then, he disappeared completely.

Chapter 47 - The families escape

It was all Daniel and Ruth could do to detach themselves from the scene. To get Jonah's family away from the furnace was almost impossible.

Jonah's mother had screamed out when Jonah had fallen into the flames. She broke free of the people trying to pull her away from the furnace room. Jonah's father and brothers ran after her and they all knelt as close as they could to the hot furnace.

The heat from the fire blasted their tears away as they called out Jonah's name in the hope that he would rise out of the fire. Nothing came out of the fire apart from red flames and white heat.

Ruth walked over to Jonah's mother, struggling with all of her own emotions, and embraced her.

'He was a hero', she said quietly.

Jonah's mother looked at Ruth, drew her closer and said, 'Thank you for saying that.'

After a moment, she pulled away from Ruth.

'What happened to him? Why wasn't he with you?' she asked.

By this time Daniel was standing beside them, looking around, wary that more soldiers would be coming. He was deeply upset about Jonah, but they still had to get out of the

Shattered Lord's castle.

'We need to go - now!' he said, hearing footsteps in the corridor.

Jonah's mother was still looking at Ruth.

'I don't know why he had turned grey. All I know is that he left us at the Glassmaker's house. That was the last time we saw him, until now. I am so sorry.'

'I'm not leaving' replied his mother.

'But he fought to give you the chance to escape. Don't squander his sacrifice', said Ruth, a trembling in her voice.

Quietly, Jonah's mother and the rest of his family stood and one by one whispered, 'Thank you, Jonah, for what you have done'. With heavy hearts, they ran towards the door that led them out of the castle.

Chapter 48 - The Glassmaker is coming

The door led them to the side of the castle and into bright sunlight and the clashing of swords. The fighting wasn't as fierce as at the front of the castle, but a way through would be difficult.

A shining one ran to them. It was Nathaniel.

Daniel and Ruth ran up to him and they embraced.

'It is so good to see you!' said Daniel.

'Looks like you need help', replied Nathaniel, looking at the line of glass people who had been rescued

A group of grey soldiers engaged them in battle. Daniel, Ruth and Nathaniel fought, as the escapees cowered at the foot of the castle. If it hadn't been for Noah and Jade joining them, they would have been overcome.

'Looks like you had found your families', said Noah, 'let's get them out of here to safety'.

'We found our friend, Jonah', said Daniel, a deep sadness evident in his face, 'He had turned grey'.

It was at that moment a blast of what sounded like a trumpet, shook the ground on which they stood. It was overwhelming and everyone instinctively looked up and put their hands over their ears. As well as the sound, there was a light that made everything else look dark. As their eyes adjusted to the light, they could see and feel a movement coming from the direction in which they had all travelled. Their bodies pulsated with life, so although what was happening was overwhelming, they were not afraid.

'What is it?' shouted Daniel.

Nathaniel looked to where the sound and light was coming from and said, 'The Glassmaker is coming!'

TO BE CONCLUDED IN
'THE GLASS PEOPLE AND THE FANTASTIC VICTORY'

Book III
The Glass People and the Fantastic Victory

Alan Kilpatrick

"I am the Way, the Truth and the Life'
(Jesus)

For Jan, Jas & Joel, Sunday, Keziah, Nathan and Rowan

Many thanks to Jan Isherwood, Darrell Cocup, Jenny Reid and Bridget Trayling for editing comments.

A story for children of all ages

Chapter 1 - The Glassmaker Arrives

The air crackled with life as the Glassmaker walked onto the battlefield. He was glorious, almost unrecognisable and terribly frightening. He came with such authority, power and life that everything else seemed to pale into insignificance, every worry seemed to fall away and whatever self-importance anyone had withered into non-existence.

The soldiers of the Shattered Lord didn't hang around and fled in fear as the Glassmaker approached. Even the splinter cats took flight, screeching like finger nails down a blackboard.

Still the Glassmaker came, loud and bright, the ground shaking. He had done nothing yet, nor had He said anything, but His presence changed the atmosphere. Each soldier felt hope rising within them and that hope erupted into cheering.

Daniel and Ruth were still by the door they had escaped through with their families and all of the other prisoners. It had been by the sacrifice of Jonah their friend, that they had escaped. The families were weak and tired, but now that the Glassmaker was arriving all of their senses were on high alert. They couldn't see all of the shining soldiers around them, as they were part of the invisible realm that could only be seen by those who had gone through the Glassmaker's furnace. For the moment, the only ones they could see were

Daniel and Ruth and the fleeing grey soldiers.

'What's happening?' cried out Daniel's father.

'Help us!' shouted his mother.

Daniel ran over to his mother and father and crouched beside them.

'Don't worry', he said to them, 'The Glassmaker is coming. That's what you can sense.'

All of the families looked at Daniel, puzzled by him speaking of the Glassmaker.

He could see their disbelief.

'The Glassmaker is real. His house is real and the furnace is real. Ruth and I chose to go through the furnace and we were forever changed. That is why we look like this now. Jonah refused to go through. He thought we were being tricked', Daniel said.

He looked at Jonah's family as he said this and then quickly looked away.

'We need to go and meet the Glassmaker', said Noah to Daniel and Ruth.

Daniel looked up at him.

'Yes we are coming', he replied.

'Who are you talking to?', asked Daniel's sister, for they could not see anyone else and it looked as though Daniel was speaking to empty space.

Daniel looked around at the army the families could not see.

'Even your eyes are changed when you go through the Glassmaker's furnace. You can see things that are invisible, but are more real than anything else', he said to Sarah, his sister.

He stepped back and looked at them all, seeing their tiredness and confusion, and said, 'Our world has been taken captive and is at war and now we are fighting to take it back!'

Chapter 2 - The Families Hear The Story

'What do you mean we are at war?' shouted someone from the back.

'We were just prisoners of a madman, and now you are talking about an invisible battle and walking into furnaces. That's mad talk!', said another

The families started to get agitated from tiredness and confusion, and were now becoming more vocal.

Ruth could see that Daniel was getting frustrated even though he had just rescued his family. His fists were clenched and a tension was apparent in his body. As the cacophony of voices grew, his frustration boiled over.

'Stop!' he yelled.

All went quiet around him. All eyes were now fixed on him. A tear appeared on his face and ran down his cheek. Ruth moved to his side and said nothing. Daniel looked at her.

'Why did Jonah have to die?' he asked sadly.

Although he spoke quietly to Ruth, everyone heard the question, including Jonah's mother and father. They both broke down in tears and sank to the ground. They had watched as Jonah fell into the furnace, defending them from the grey soldiers. He had given his life to enable them to escape.

Ruth's mother and father moved to them and comforted the couple in the despair of losing their son. Ruth looked imploringly at Daniel, trying to will him to go over to Jonah's parents and support them, but he just remained where he was. He looked over at Noah, who was still unseen by the families. He asked the question again: 'Why did the Glassmaker let Jonah die?'

Noah stayed silent.

For a short while the families had forgotten about their fear as they helped and supported Jonah's family, but eventually the fear crept in and anxiety rose.

Peter, Daniel's father, approached Daniel and put his hand on his shoulder. He spoke gently to him.

'Son, we are all confused and frightened. Please tell us what is going on? You have freed us, but it felt safer in prison. Freedom is scary when you don't know what is happening or you have no control.'

Daniel looked at his father, a turmoil of emotions tumbling through his heart. It was Ruth who responded.

'We were on the top of Knock Hill when the grey soldiers attacked and took you all prisoners. It all seems so long ago…' she paused, thinking of her previous life.

Daniel spoke at last and continued what Ruth had started:

'We were helpless and distraught, so we did what we could. We embarked on a journey that didn't seem sensible to the Glassmaker's house. It was a journey that changed us forever. It was difficult, but eventually we made it to the house and discovered that the Glassmaker and his furnace was real.'

There was a sharp intake of breath from some of the people listening, people who had been brought up to believe that the Glassmaker and his furnace was just a fairy tale.

Ruth moved and stood beside Daniel.

'We met the Glassmaker and He told us that the only way

we could help you was to go through his furnace', she paused, and looked at Daniel, 'We made the decision to go through it and when we came out we looked like this. We had been healed. All of our cracks had been mended. We could also see the battle that has been going on, but can't be seen and we decided to fight and do everything possible to find you and help you.'

By this time the families had started to gather around them, including Jonah's father and mother.

Jonah's father, edged to the front.

'What happened to Jonah?' he asked.

Daniel and Ruth looked at each other.

'Jonah didn't trust the Glassmaker and refused to go through the furnace. He ran out of the house and that was the last we saw of him until now', answered Ruth.

Jonah's mother burst into tears again and her husband put his arms round her. All the others looked at the ground and said nothing.

Ruth took Daniel by the arm and guided him to where Noah and the troop were standing silently.

She looked at Daniel and spoke sharply to him, 'What on earth are you doing? What is happening to you? We have just rescued our families and all you can do is question the Glassmaker! Jonah made his choice.'

Jade came and stood beside Daniel.

'Your families are safe. I am sorry about your friend, but you have something to be thankful for', she said to him.

'Really', said Daniel sarcastically, 'I just watched my friend die and you think I should be thankful!'

Ruth, Nathaniel, Noah and Jade all tensed up and were looking behind Daniel.

'Yes', boomed the voice of the Glassmaker, 'There is always something to be thankful for!'

Chapter 3 - The Families Meet The Glassmaker

Daniel stiffened at the voice of the Glassmaker and slowly turned around to face him. The Glassmaker now looked as He had done when Daniel had first met him at his house. A regal, old man with a bushy white beard. He was unable to look the Glassmaker in the eye.

'Look at me', said the Glassmaker in a gentle, but firm voice.

Daniel slowly lifted his eyes and looked at the Glassmaker. The Glassmaker said nothing and held Daniel's gaze. Standing there, in the full gaze of the Glassmaker, Daniel felt uncomfortable.

'Please stop!' he said.

'Stop what?' asked the Glassmaker.

'Looking at me. It's uncomfortable', said Daniel.

'Why would my gaze be uncomfortable to you?' asked the Glassmaker.

Daniel didn't reply, but deep inside, in a secret place, doubts were taking root.

The conversation was interrupted by Peter, Daniel's father.

'Who are you talking to this time?' he asked.

The Glassmaker continued to look at Daniel and then moved his gaze to Ruth.

'I am going to let your families see me briefly and I will

explain a little. It will be frightening for them, but the fear will pass and courage will start to creep into them', He said to Ruth.

The air around them all started to shimmer and move. Very subtly at first, but then growing in intensity. The families didn't see anything initially, but then one of them called out, 'What's that? What's happening?' He was pointing at the vibrating air.

There were one or two screams and they started to move away.

'Don't be afraid!', said Ruth

'What's happening', asked her mother.

'The Glassmaker is coming', she replied.

'What? I don't understand!', she said to Ruth, but her eyes were transfixed on the place that was distorting and shimmering.

'You are frightening them!' said Daniel, but the Glassmaker remained silent.

The families saw an increasing brightness appearing. It grew in intensity so that they had to shield their eyes. Light exploded all around them and then it disappeared. In front of them stood the Glassmaker. The Glassmaker smiled at them and said, 'I am the Glassmaker and all things will be well.'

'You're real!' stuttered Peter.

'I believe so', said the Glassmaker, smiling, 'don't be afraid. I am for you and I fight for you. There is a battle going on all around you, even now. But, all will be well. Trust Daniel and Ruth and have faith in me.'

Nobody said anything. They were overcome with the revelation that the Glassmaker was real and He was standing in front of them.

He looked at them all, smiled again and said, 'We will meet again.'

With those words, He faded into the invisible realm. The eyes and hearts of the families searched for understanding, but none came. They hadn't yet realised that some things could not be understood, but could only be accessed by faith. Peter looked at Daniel and Ruth and said, 'We believe. What do we need to do?'

Chapter 4 - Ramiel's Rantings

Whilst the Glassmaker was talking to the families, the Shattered Lord paced up and down his throne room shouting and screaming at the Glassmaker to get his attention.

'Look at me! Listen to me!' he ranted, but the Glassmaker did not acknowledge him.

The Shattered Lord's Castle was a hive of bustling activity as grey soldiers tried to find out what was happening. They didn't have any information and that lack of information and communication started to breed fear. They hustled and bumped into each other and arguments soon broke out and splinter cats flew around in confusion and disarray. Many of the grey soldiers had once been friends and servants of the Glassmaker, but they had been caught up in the rebellion between the Glassmaker and Ramiel. They had been expelled from his presence and now they were living a sort of twilight life with no presence or remembrance of joy. They lived a half-life existence, following rules and to all intents and purposes were slaves. Their lives seemed to consist of being shouted at and shouting at others. The castle was not a place of peace. The rest of the grey soldiers had once been glass people who had either refused to trust the Glassmaker or had been captured by the Shattered Lord and forced to serve him. It was this disparate and unhappy mob that frenetically scurried around the castle like a colony of ants.

The problem was that they were trapped in the castle. As soon as the Shattered Lord saw that the Glassmaker was coming he spoke out some incoherent words and a force field that crackled and sparked started to appear above them and had gradually enveloped the whole castle. As soon as the grey soldiers realised what was happening they all ran back to the safety of the castle. Most made it in time, but some grey soldiers were trapped outside the crackling force field and were promptly taken prisoner by the Glassmaker's army.

Nobody dared go near the Shattered Lord as anyone who did was smashed into pieces by his hand. Even his closest friend, Tabbris, stood out of reach of Ramiel's destructive hand.

'So you think you can beat me! You dare to come into my kingdom and challenge me! You have not changed. You are uncaring and deceptive. What if all of your soldiers knew the truth? Do you think they would still serve you? Where's your angelic host? Are they too scared of me? I see you are sacrificing the transformed and deluded glass people. Typical of you to sacrifice the very people you created!'

And so he went on and on, not stopping in his horrible accusations and taunting.

Eventually Tabbris felt brave enough to ask Ramiel a question.

'What are your orders, my lord?' he asked, bowing so low that his deformed forehead nearly touched the floor.

'My orders are that you destroy the Glassmaker! My orders are that you fight! My orders are that you bring me victory!' he snarled.

'How should I do that?' asked Tabbris timidly.

The Shattered Lord paused in his ranting. Tabbris didn't lift his head in case it was hit by Ramiel, but he did lift his eyes and saw that Ramiel had stopped pacing. Tabbris slowly lifted his head and saw that Ramiel's face had changed. Was that fear he saw on Ramiel's face? Tabbris followed the gaze of Ramiel to see what he was being transfixed by. He understood why. The Glassmaker was looking directly at the Shattered Lord.

Chapter 5 - The Glassmaker And Ramiel Talk

Although the Shattered Lord wanted the Glassmaker to pay attention to him, he had forgotten the intensity of that attention. Here was purity and a goodness that felt painful to Ramiel. He took a step back and, for the first time in a long while, he felt intimidated. That was not the intention of the Glassmaker. Goodness and purity can be intimidating to those who are not good or pure.

'Ramiel, it has been a long time', said the Glassmaker.

Everyone behind the fizzling barrier of crackled glass was in awe of the Glassmaker and they could see that Ramiel was clearly disconcerted by this power. They had not seen each other since the rebellion and Ramiel had forgotten how glorious the Glassmaker was.

'It's good to see you', continued the Glassmaker, his eyes filled with compassion.

The eyes of love were too much for Ramiel and made him feel sick. All the anger and fury within Ramiel exploded in a vicious torrent of abuse aimed at the Glassmaker.

'You betrayed me! You didn't love me as you should have done and I reject any love, any compassion that you have for me. I reject you and all your creation!' he snarled.

As he was venting, Ramiel's body distorted. The room around him succumbed to the fury that was being released.

Tabbris was at the far end of the throne room and Ramiel's fury was creating cracks all over his body and all who were standing in the room. The grey soldiers and splinter cats trapped in the castle found dark hiding places wherever they could.

The Glassmaker just stood still, watching Ramiel. He hadn't finished yet.

'I will do anything and everything to bring you down, to defeat you, to crush you, to make you feel the pain that you caused me. I will crack you and distort you!'

By this time Ramiel was yelling at the top of his voice. The cracking of glass was deafening and the pain that Ramiel was causing was increasing in all who were near him.

Tabbris cried out in pain, 'Ramiel! Stop, please!'

The cry distracted Ramiel from the Glassmaker for a moment and Ramiel looked at Tabbris and the chaos that his anger was causing. He didn't regret inflicting pain, even on those who were supposed to be on his side. Ramiel saw Tabbris not so much as a friend, or even a servant, but as a slave. They had been friends once, but no more. Ramiel felt he had been betrayed by the Glassmaker and that supposed betrayal had filled him with anger and distrust and pain. Ramiel believed that everyone should feel how he felt and so he didn't mind seeing Tabbris writhing on the floor in pain.

The Glassmaker's voice focused Ramiel's attention once again on the centre of all his hatred.

'Why do you erect walls around you?' asked the Glassmaker.

Ramiel looked at the force field surrounding his castle.

'To protect me from your horrible compassion and goodness!' he replied.

'But they don't protect you from anything', responded the Glassmaker, 'You have simply created your own prison!'

Chapter 6 - Daniel's Doubt

As the Shattered Lord was shouting at the Glassmaker, Fleck, Oswald and Albert, joined Daniel, Ruth, Noah, Nathaniel and Jade.

'What is the Glassmaker going to do?' growled Fleck.

'I don't know', replied Nathaniel, 'but the Shattered Lord is not going to surrender.'

'There will be more fighting', said Albert, 'It always ends in fighting.'

Daniel stayed silent in the conversation that was going on. He fixed his attention on the Glassmaker, who was calmly watching the Shattered Lord, as Ramiel distorted and cracked and caused pain in the castle.

'Why is the Glassmaker hurting the Shattered Lord? Doesn't He see that He is causing pain to everyone in the castle', thought Daniel.

At that moment Ramiel stopped shouting and looked directly at Daniel, who he could see far off in the distance. It was as though Ramiel could read Daniel's mind.

'Why is he looking at you?' asked Ruth.

'I don't know', said Daniel, worrying that he had said his previous thoughts aloud.

The Glassmaker's gaze turned towards Daniel. A sadness was in the Glassmaker's eyes, as if He also knew what Daniel was thinking.

Oswald, who had been perching on a tree, flew down to Daniel's side.

'It will be okay', he said to Daniel.

'Will it?' replied Daniel.

'Of course it will', said Ruth.

Daniel looked at Ruth, turned and walked away to another part of the camp.

Fleck looked at Ruth.

'What's wrong with him?' he asked gruffly.

'I really don't know', said Ruth.

'Doubt', said Oswald.

'What!' said Ruth.

'Daniel is experiencing doubt. He is choosing to walk by doubt, rather than trust the Glassmaker', continued Oswald.

Ruth looked at the Glassmaker.

He walked over to Ruth and said, 'All will be well.'

Chapter 7 - Beautiful Tabbris

'There you go again', shouted Ramiel to the Glassmaker, as he watched Daniel separate from his friends.

'You have a gift of creating discord and disunity! You have not changed', he continued.

The Glassmaker responded, breaking his silence.

'You mistake someone thinking through what they see and hear and 'active rebellion'. You can walk a questioning path and still end at a place of faith and love. It doesn't always have to end up in turning against your creator', said the Glassmaker.

'Ha!' said the Shattered Lord, 'I accept that you created me, but I choose the right to question and then rebel. It is my joy to do that! It is the best thing I have ever done; I have created my own destiny, my own kingdom and I will make sure as many as possible join my kingdom - whether they want to or not.'

The Glassmaker once again stayed silent and turned his gaze to Tabbris, who was cowering in the shadows.

'Beautiful Tabbris', he said.

Ramiel laughed loudly, 'Him?! Beautiful?!'

The light of the Glassmaker burned brighter for a moment and Ramiel had to turn his face away.

'Yes, he is beautiful, Ramiel. I made him. I know him. I

love him. I look on the inside and beauty is deep within him.'

'No!' cried out Ramiel, 'He is not beautiful. He is repulsive, rebellious and obnoxious, and you made him that way!'

Poor Tabbris tried to squeeze into a darker place so he was not the centre of attention. He didn't want them arguing about him, but he felt deeply moved by the words of the Glassmaker. In the most secret place of his heart, he hid the truth that he shared with no-one: he regretted joining with Ramiel. He had honestly thought that the Glassmaker was hurting Ramiel long ago in the Glassmaker's throne room. However, over time he came to see that the Glassmaker was good and that knowledge made him feel even worse when the Glassmaker spoke to him. He wished he now hated the Glassmaker as he thought it might make it easier for him. But hate wasn't working for him. He didn't hate the Glassmaker and his choices had departed him from his creator.

'Stop whimpering in the shadows', Ramiel said to Tabbris meanly.

He looked at the Glassmaker once more.

'See, you are still causing us pain. You are still the same creator bully and I will destroy you!'

Chapter 8 - The First Tree Returns

What Tabbris didn't know was that the anger and fury in Ramiel covered up a broken heart that had hardened and shrunk after so many years of hatred. That's what happens when someone shouts at us, or criticises us, or dislikes us. It becomes a pain deep inside us, not because of something we have done. Our outward act is triggered by our broken heart. That was what was happening to Ramiel.

The brokenness in Ramiel also increased his pride. He felt he was right and he felt he was justified in his wrath and as a result he created a wall of pride around him. He couldn't show weakness. He couldn't admit that he had been or was now wrong. If only he had accepted and understood that there was a way of healing and reconciliation. But if that thought had ever entered his mind, even for a millisecond, the wall of pride hardened and solidified and his resolve to destroy the Glassmaker strengthened.

'Come, first tree', Ramiel commanded.

As the words echoed around the castle, the floor in his throne room started to shake and crack and break up. Out of the floor emerged small branches that grew at an alarming rate. Spheres appeared on the branches, as they had done in the desert. The first tree grew to full size, dominating the room.

Daniel and Ruth looked on and recognised the tree that had tempted them and they knew that the spheres were glass people who had succumbed to temptation and were trapped. All around the castle, grey soldiers and splinter cats watched the tree as it grew. The spheres on the branches didn't remain spheres. They turned into glass people, hanging on the branches, helpless and so, so miserable. The strange thing was that even though the tree was holding them captive, they also held onto the tree and didn't want to let go. They looked as though all hope had left them. When it feels that all hope has left, you believe that it is not worth living and that is how the hanging people felt. They had made their choices and were now living with the consequences.

Everyone was in the Glassmaker's army were now focused on the tree and its sorry looking attachments. Within each shining soldier the sight stirred up a feeling of compassion and anger. Compassion for the glass people without hope, anger at Ramiel and the first tree for creating that despair.

'This is the first tree', declared the Shattered Lord, 'and with its help I will destroy the Glassmaker and all who support him. Just for fun let's add another piece of fruit to the tree.'

At these words the tree shook gently and one of the grey soldiers in the throne room started to weep.

'No! No!' he cried, 'not that.'

What he meant by 'not that' no-one was sure, but they saw the soldier walk helplessly to the tree, which promptly picked him up by a branch. The soldier hung there and howled and wailed and all the others on the tree joined in, creating a discordant cacophony.

All around covered their ears and it brought many shining ones to their knees. After a short time Ramiel told it to stop and there was silence.

'You can't destroy me', countered the Glassmaker.

'Maybe not, but I can destroy all your people and, in the process, hurt your heart!'

Ramiel was shouting once again. He then uttered strange words and called forth the four fires of destruction.

'No', cried the Glassmaker softly, 'Don't misuse the fires.' Distress was etched on his face.

The first tree shuddered and from the bottom of its trunk fire started to emerge and climb up its trunk, consuming the tree as the fire rose. The glass people hanging on the tree cried out in fear and every part of the tree, including the people, was consumed with fire. There was an explosion and from the four main branches light shot out to the east and west, north and south. Everyone looked up at the sky and saw the fiery lights extend to the farthest horizon. In the four corners of the kingdom four great fires came into being and they rose to the sky turning it red. The fires of destructions started their journey of chaos. Nothing was left of the first tree or the hanging glass people.

Ramiel smiled and said, 'Destruction comes.'

A tear fell down the face of the Glassmaker.

Chapter 9 - The Families And The Fires

Of course the families couldn't see all that was happening, but they did sense something was wrong. This was confirmed when light suddenly exploded in the sky and flew in four different directions. Constable Bunce was knocked to the floor by the explosion and several people yelled in fright. There was no cover around to which they could run, so they all crowded together and found comfort in being near each other. Ruth ran up to them.

'Are you alright?' she asked, looking around at each one of them and then up at the sky.

'I think so', replied Constable Bunce stoically, picking himself up from the floor, 'but what on earth is happening?'

By this time Daniel arrived, and the rest of the troop approached unseen by the families. Ruth looked at Daniel with a quizzical look as if to say, 'What on earth is going on with you?', but she said no words aloud. She could see that he was not in the right frame of mind to talk about it, so she continued to help the families.

'I know it seems incredibly confusing and uncertain', she said, 'It will feel like the ground is shaking under your feet and there is nothing to hold onto in order to steady yourself. I understand that you want to have answers, and they will come I'm sure, but just not now.'

'Why not now?' asked one of the people, who happened to be from Knock and Ruth recognised him, 'We deserve to know.'

Ruth could see frustration bubbling up in the hearts of the families and she understood why, with all that had gone on, and now was going on. Ruth turned to Daniel.

'You say something.'

It was more of a command rather than a suggestion and Daniel resented it. He looked at her and then at his family and then back at Ruth.

'I…I can't', he replied, 'sorry.'

He turned and walked away. What Ruth and the families didn't know was that Ramiel had begun planting seeds of doubt and words of discouragement into the soft heart of Daniel and instead of ignoring them, he started to listen to them.

'What's wrong with Daniel?' asked Sarah, his sister.

Ruth was distracted for a moment, but Sarah's question brought her attention back to the families.

'All will be well', she said, echoing the words of the Glassmaker.

'Will it?' said Sarah, her eyes following Daniel as he walked away.

Chapter 10 - The Invisible Becomes Visible

The four fires of destruction were well named. They grew in heat and destroyed everything in their paths. They had appeared far, far away, but they started to move slowly back to the place where they had originated, the Shattered Lord's Castle, burning and melting everything in their paths. The only person who could survive the fires was the Glassmaker. Ramiel thought that the forcefield that now surrounded his castle might protect him from the fires, but he wasn't sure. He was so intent on destroying the Glassmaker that he would take the risk. He didn't care if he was melted. His sole purpose was to cause the Glassmaker pain.

In the distant villages of the Glass Kingdom the fires approached and started to do their horrible work of misery. In the distant villages of Kitpuddle and Droop the fires began to burn and melt houses as the desperate villagers, not understanding what was happening, tried to escape to safety. Not all of them made it. Not that the fires, or Ramiel cared in the slightest. They were both doing their jobs of creating fear, pain and chaos. If only Ramiel had remembered what he was created for and not allowed anger and pain to twist and distort him.

In the southern edges of the Kingdom, the villages of Throop and Didling, people were at their workplaces and schools, going about their usual business, when the fires crashed in on them. The screams of adults and children filled the air as the poor people tried to run for safety.

The Glassmaker was aware of what was happening, and the actions of Ramiel had unsettled the Glassmaker's army. Daniel had made his way back to the side of the Glassmaker.

'What's going on?' he asked the Glassmaker.

The Glassmaker looked at Daniel and spoke a single word: 'destruction'.

'What!', cried out Daniel.

For the first time since he had been transformed by the furnace, Daniel felt afraid of the Glassmaker. He had let doubt and anger seep into his heart. The Glassmaker started to grow and glow with light. Everyone cowered, no knowing whether they were now more afraid of the fires or of the Glassmaker.

The air shimmered and pulsated as the Glassmaker shone and sung with such beauty and power. As the air vibrated to the tune of the Glassmaker, the glass people in every part of the Kingdom started to realise that they were not alone. The Glassmaker was singing over them. They started to see the invisible world that had surrounded them, all of their lives. They saw shining ones helping people escape to safety and protect many from the fires. They were afraid of what they saw, but they all felt hope rising.

Chapter 11 - The Glassmaker Is Not Good

Daniel had run off as this was all happening. He was so confused and many different emotions were swirling around his head and heart. He ran near to the castle, to the bottom of the thrumming force-field and found a spot where no-one could see him. Or at least he thought no-one could see him. Ramiel looked down from his throne room and saw that Daniel had run away from the Glassmaker and had tried to hide. He saw and felt Daniel's confusion.

'Well, well', he thought, as he watched and waited.

Daniel sat on a rock beside a tree and hung his head. His thoughts were jumbled and his heart was hurting. He knew in his head what he should think, but his heart was saying something different. He was angry. So angry. Why had the Glassmaker allowed Jonah to die? He could not stop asking that question. Why did the Glassmaker not intervene and stop the horrors of seeing his friend sink into the furnace? Jonah had only made one bad choice as far as Daniel could see and Daniel felt that Jonah was being punished for that choice. Even Jonah had seen the error of his ways. He had realised that he had made a wrong choice in rejecting the Glassmaker and had sacrificed himself for his friends. Why had it ended in the death of Jonah?

Ramiel saw his chance and slipped into the thoughts of

Daniel and whispered, 'Do you see where the threads of your thoughts lead you? The Glassmaker is not all good. He lets you down and lets your friends down. That is why I couldn't serve him anymore. I saw through him and his deceit.'

Daniel's eyes roved around as though trying to search for a different conclusion or a different way of seeing the situation. But he couldn't.

'He has disappointed you', Ramiel said quietly and waited for the dark thought to break Daniel.

But no crack appeared.

'I will break you', thought Ramiel and he withdrew into the shadows of Daniel's mind.

Chapter 12 - The Glassmaker And Laughter

Ruth was standing slightly apart from her family. They were still unsure of her even though the battle had been revealed. However, when someone changes so drastically it can be difficult for family and friends to adjust to the change. She had not seen Daniel for a while.

'I am sure he is okay', she thought to herself.

In this time of battle and uncertainty she wanted to be near her family.

As she looked at her family, she could see that they were tense and unsettled by what was happening. She was about to go over to them and to try and comfort them when she saw the Glassmaker approach them. They all stood, wary of his approach. Children hid behind their parents and the fathers moved in front of their families. The Glassmaker stopped when he saw their reaction, but He did not turn and leave. He didn't get angry with them. He didn't belittle them. He simply looked at them and smiled. Ruth had seen that smile after she and Daniel had walked through the furnace. They had emerged completely healed and transformed and as they had walked up out of the furnace the Glassmaker had smiled. It was a smile that brought hope to whoever saw it. All around was the cacophony of an army getting ready for battle and the pulsing of the force-field circling the castle. But in that smile the Glassmaker had created an oasis of security and peace for the families and Ruth loved Him all the more for that. Her heart was bursting with thankfulness for Him and she was about to go up to the Glassmaker when she saw one of the children step from behind their parents. The child paused for a moment and then ran up to the Glassmaker, who knelt down with arms wide open into which the child raced. They embraced and more children ran to Him. They knocked Him over with their exuberance and they rolled on the ground and laughed, just as Ruth and Daniel had done at their transformation. It was an infectious laugh and soon the parents realised and one to two of them started to smile and then join in on the laughter. The Glassmaker eventually sat up, looked at the adults and said, 'All will be well.'

Ruth's father nodded back at the Glassmaker, turned and looked at his daughter, walked over to her and wrapped his arms around her.

'I love you', he said.

Ruth looked at the smiling Glassmaker and a tear of joy ran down her cheek.

Chapter 13 - The Glassmaker Can't Be Trusted

Ramiel once again crept into Daniel's mind and tried to wrap his broken words around Daniel's thoughts. Daniel's face darkened as he listened to the doubts and lies being conjured up by Ramiel.

'If the Glassmaker let Jonah die, then why not you or Ruth?' Ramiel said.

Daniel thought for a moment.

'He wouldn't let that happen. He wouldn't do that to us! He just helped free my family. Why would He let them die?' replied Daniel, his thoughts starting to twist a little. He was beginning to get confused and Ramiel was stoking the embers of anger that had appeared.

'Why wouldn't he?' replied Ramiel unhelpfully.

'Because He wouldn't!' stammered Daniel. He had no other response as doubt was digging up the roots of his faith in the Glassmaker. Tears started to well up.

'He wouldn't...he wouldn't do that!' said Daniel, wavering in his convictions. Ramiel saw the doubt growing and delighted in it.

'The Glassmaker is not to be honoured, but feared. He does everything for his own benefit, not yours. Not mine. Look at me Daniel, look at what the Glassmaker did to me.'

Daniel didn't look.

'Look at me!' demanded Ramiel.

Slowly, in his thoughts, Daniel raised his head and looked at Ramiel. He was repulsed by what he saw.

'The Glassmaker did this to me. He made me this way and then threw me out of his presence because He didn't like the way I looked', said Ramiel gently, feigning sadness.

'I can't.. I can't believe that', stuttered Daniel.

'You can't believe that He would do that? Look at what He did to your friend! Look at what He did to me - what more evidence do you need! Do your eyes deceive you?' shouted Ramiel

Ramiel cracked a little as his anger rose and Daniel cowered in the corner of his mind, not wanting to believe any of it, but finding that he was slipping down a slope away from trusting the Glassmaker.

Chapter 14 - Ruth Sees Daniel Struggling

The Glassmaker walked over to Ruth. Even in the midst of this horrendous war, he made time for her. She was sitting on the ground with her family and stood up as He approached.

'Walk with me', invited the Glassmaker.

He offered a hand and she took it. They walked to the top of a small hill that afforded them a view of the whole situation. Ramiel's castle stood seemingly invulnerable. She could see activity on the ramparts of the castle. All of the prison cells in the walls were open, but empty. Nothing could be seen of what was happening inside the castle. She looked at the Glassmaker's army as it scuttled around finding the best positions for defence and attack, making sure that the rescued people were protected and safe.

She looked at the sky and in the distance she could see the red glow of the approaching fires conjured up by Ramiel. She could see that they were getting closer and her heart went out to all the people in the kingdom who had to leave all they knew to escape the impending danger.

She turned to look at the Glassmaker. He stood silently, looking at someone at the base of the castle wall, just outside the castle's defensive shield. His gaze was fixed on the person, who was walking back and forth. It looked like they were talking or shouting to themselves. As her eyes adjusted, she realised that it was Daniel. She was taken aback that the light shining from him had dulled and there was worry and anger etched on his face.

'Daniel…' she started to shout as she moved towards him, but the Glassmaker put his hand on her forearm and stilled her.

'He is listening to the wrong voice', He said, 'he is allowing Ramiel into his thoughts.'

'What! Why would he do that?' cried out Ruth.

'He is in pain and pain makes us do unexpected things', replied the Glassmaker.

'Can't you stop his pain?' asked Ruth, still looking at Daniel.

'I have the power to, but is that what he wants?' said the Glassmaker.

Ruth looked at him.

'I don't understand'.

The Glassmaker moved his gaze from Daniel to Ruth.

'Sometimes we use pain as a shield to help us not to face the truth.'

'What truth?' asked Ruth.

'The truth that Jonah died. He thinks I punished Jonah for not going through the furnace. He can't see that Ramiel has caused this and that I am redeeming all things. The way I do things can seem strange to people.'

He paused for a moment and looked back at Daniel.

'But I do know what I am doing.'

'What does redeem mean?'

The Glassmaker looked tenderly back at Ruth.

'It means to buy back all that was lost', He replied.

Ruth thought for a moment.

'What will it cost?' she asked.

Once again the Glassmaker smiled. That smile that transformed how you thought and felt. That smile that was like a ray of sunshine breaking from behind a cloud.

'Daniel will need your help. He has to go further away in order to come back.'

And with those words the Glassmaker walked away, leaving Ruth watching her restless friend.

Chapter 15 - I Will Never Lie To You

'Do you think you are loved?' asked Ramiel, 'Do you even know what that means?'

Daniel was walking by the edge of the shield. On the other side he could see the broken image of Ramiel.

'Why won't you leave me alone?' cried out Daniel. 'Stop following me!'

Ramiel smiled as he could see the desperation and doubt growing within Daniel.

'The Glassmaker does love me', said Daniel, his voice filled with uncertainty, 'He made me like new. He mended my cracks.'

Ramiel laughed, 'He loves to see people crack and break. That is why He mends them. He wants to prolong the pain.'

Daniel turned in anger and slammed his fists against the shield sending little ripples in the wall. He stared at Ramiel, unsure whether to believe him or not. A short while ago he would have attacked Ramiel, as he was a traitor, but now he was having a conversation with him, listening to what he was saying. How quickly faith moves to doubt and doubt changes our mind and perceptions. Ramiel approached the wall and placed his hands where Daniel's were.

'I will never lie to you or let you down', he said.

'Why should I believe you? You destroy people for your

own use.'

Ramiel's eyes widened and more cracks appeared on his face and then he disappeared from Daniel's sight.

Chapter 16 - Daniel And Oswald

Perched on a tree nearby, Oswald the owl looked down on Daniel. He had watched the whole scene play out, but he had not seen Ramiel as he had only been in Daniel's thoughts. He had, however, seen Daniel's restlessness and had heard him talking to someone, but Oswald did not know to whom. Oswald had determined to intervene.

He flew down and landed on a rock near Daniel. It took a few moments for Daniel to be aware of Oswald's presence, he was so engrossed in his thoughts.

Daniel looked pale, his light fading, and he was stooped over, continually looking at the ground. He was in a very dark place in his thoughts and that was reflected in his physical appearance.

Daniel eventually saw Oswald, but said nothing to him. He just stared angrily.

'Hello Daniel', said Oswald cheerfully.

Daniel just grunted. It was obvious that he didn't want to be interrupted, but Oswald persisted, 'Who were you talking to?'

'No-one', came the gruff reply, 'I wasn't talking to anyone.'

'Yes, I can see that there is nobody here, but you were talking to someone. Was it Ramiel?' asked Oswald.

At the name of Ramiel, Daniel tensed and said, rather

aggressively, 'No!'

Oswald said nothing. After a period of silence Daniel spoke.

'I was just thinking about the Glassmaker, about whether He was all that good really. After all, He did let Jonah die. That proves his love is temporary. He does everything for himself and his own benefit, not ours.'

Daniel was getting louder as he spoke.

'That is not true. That is just Ramiel talking!' countered Oswald.

Daniel immediately responded, 'See, even you have been deluded as well. I think Jonah had the right idea when he ran out of the Glassmaker's house and said that the Glassmaker was not good.'

'He is good!' said Oswald. 'He is always good.'

'You believe what you want, but I am leaving this place and getting as far away as possible from the Glassmaker', said Daniel as he turned and started to walk away.

'No', said Oswald as he flew in front of Daniel.

Oswald hovered as Daniel stood still. All at once Daniel threw out his arm, knocked Oswald to the ground and ran into the hills.

Chapter 17 - Ruth Tries To Find Daniel

Ruth had been sitting with her family, enjoying being with them as they talked with excitement about the Glassmaker and the revelation of the invisible battle. It seemed out of place to sit with her family as the stalemate continued between the Shattered Lord's army, the impending fires and the Glassmaker's army, but because of those things and the uncertainty of the future she wanted to cherish each moment with her family.

She was looking around and saw that Daniel was no longer at the bottom of the castle wall. Jade was passing by and Ruth called out to her.

'Jade, have you seen Daniel?'

'No, I haven't', shouted back Jade as she continued to pass by, 'maybe he is with Noah.'

Ruth stood up and looked for Noah. Not seeing him, she started to walk away from her family. Her mother looked up.

'Where are you going, sweetheart?'

Ruth looked at her mother and then went back to searching for Daniel.

'I can't see Daniel anywhere and I'm worried about him', she said.

Her mother stood up and went to her daughter's side.

'Go and find him', she said to Ruth.

This was the encouragement she needed. She didn't want to leave her family so soon, but she was very worried about Daniel. He had been acting so strangely and had not spent any time with his family. Ruth went to her mother and kissed her on the forehead.

'Thank you.'

She smiled at her mother and then ran off.

Concern was growing within her about Daniel and he needed to be found. He was distant and had started looking at the Glassmaker warily. He had been sullen and moody the last time she had seen him and she wasn't sure why.

She ran through the multitude of shining ones, calling out for Noah, Jade, or Nathaniel. Finally, she saw Noah through a crowd of soldiers and she pushed her way through them. She arrived beside him breathless.

'Have you seen Daniel? I'm worried about him', she asked.

'Not for a while', Noah replied. 'Last time I saw him he was brooding, for some reason, at the base of the barrier near a group of trees. We need you both. Remember you are supposed to be leading.'

Ruth said 'I know' and 'thanks' and ran off to the base of the castle. She knew the copse that Noah had meant and made her way to it. Daniel was nowhere to be seen. Disappointed, she looked around.

'He has gone', came a voice out of nowhere.

Startled. Ruth looked upward, drawn by the direction of the voice and saw Oswald perched on the tree. He looked disheveled and ruffled.

'What happened to you?' she asked, 'What do you mean he has gone?'

'I mean what I said. He has gone, left, departed. And the reason I look like this is because I tried to stop him and he didn't like it.'

'What?! Why on earth would he do that? He has no reason to leave or harm you', Ruth said.

'He listened to the voice of the Shattered Lord and let doubt and fear enter his heart.' said Oswald, 'He is losing faith'.

Chapter 18 - Ruth Follows Daniel

After what Oswald had told her, Ruth was very concerned about Daniel. She looked around anxiously as though she would be able to see a solution.

'What's wrong, Ruth?' a voice said behind her.

She was startled and turned quickly to see who was speaking. It was the Glassmaker.

'Where did you…'

She didn't finish her sentence as it didn't matter where He had come from. All that mattered was that He was here.

'Daniel has disappeared. I don't know where he has gone. Oswald said something about him listening to the voice of the Shattered Lord and being filled with doubt and fear, but I don't know how that is possible in a shining one.'

Her words tumbled out quickly. The Glassmaker didn't say anything.

'How can that happen! I don't understand.' Worry and frustration shaping her words and how they came out.

The Glassmaker looked towards Ramiel's castle and then back at Ruth.

'Every moment is a choice. Every thought can lead to a decision. You can choose to love. You can choose not to love. You can choose to go left. You can choose to go right. You can choose to listen to my words. You can choose to listen to the words of Ramiel. Every decision, every choice you make has a consequence. If you listen to my words you become stronger, you shine brighter. If you choose to listen to the words of Ramiel, you may crack again and the light within you dims', said the Glassmaker.

He continued, 'In life there are two parallel paths. On one you walk by faith and trust. One you walk by doubt and fear. It is so easy to hop over from one path to another. Listen to Ramiel and you walk on the path of doubt and fear. Listen to me and you are on your faith walk. On each path you are still on a journey, but on one you grow brighter and on the other you fade.'

'Is..is Daniel lost forever?' asked Ruth, the beginning of tears evident in her eyes.

'No, not at all', replied the Glassmaker, bending down and cupping Ruth's face in his hands, 'he just needs to be found again. He needs to remember that I love him.'

'I'll go. Send me to find him. Please!' said Ruth.

The Glassmaker released Ruth's face and stood up to his full height. Ruth heard a noise behind her and she turned swiftly, sword in hand, only to be confronted with Noah, Nathaniel, and Jade.

'You can go!' said Noah.

'But not alone', said Jade. 'We are coming with you!'

Chapter 19 - A Journey To Find Daniel

Ruth was glad that she was not going alone. She had been terrified at the thought of leaving the safety of the Glassmaker, even though they were in the middle of a battlefield. Being near him just felt safe. Having friends go with her gave her strength.

The Glassmaker looked at each of the brave friends.

'Be strong and very courageous. Do not fear. Now go and recover the lost sheep!'

Jade, Noah, Nathaniel and Ruth looked at one another and turned to go in the direction they thought he went.

'How long will this take?' someone asked.

'I don't know', replied another.

'Where has he gone?'

'I don't know!'

'Is he still shining?'

'I don't know!'

'Do we have anything to eat?' said Nathaniel.

Everyone stopped and looked at Nathaniel.

'Searching is hungry work. I just wanted to make sure that we didn't starve before we found Daniel', said Nathaniel, smiling.

There was a moment's silence and then Noah burst out laughing.

'Yes, we have food', he said. 'Now let's find Daniel together.'

The terrain they trekked over was rocky and undulating. Here and there small shrubs grew, but other than those, the landscape was bare of vegetation. The sun shone, but the wind blew dust into their faces and made the journey difficult. For three days they walked, sleeping in the cold under the stars. On the third day grass started to appear and the ground started to slope upwards. Looking up they saw a cave high up in the hill. There seemed to be a glow coming from it.

'Let's sleep there tonight', said Nathaniel, 'it will make a change from sleeping in the open and a fire in the cave may actually create some warmth for us at night'.

'Why is the cave glowing?' asked Ruth. 'Maybe Daniel is in there!'

Ramiel had, from the safety of his castle, watched all that had gone on. Tabbris was standing silently in the corner of the throne room, afraid to move or say anything.

'I want him stopped!' said Ramiel. 'If he will not bow down to me I will melt him down and use his liquified remains to make me stronger. If he recovers from his doubt he will be too full of hope and will be stronger. He'll inspire everyone else and we can't let that happen, can we Tabbris?'

Tabbris didn't say anything.

'Can we!' shouted Ramiel

'No', said Tabbris, tentatively.

'Send some splinter cats to follow him. Wait until he has found the fruit from the second tree and then destroy him, the tree and the fruit! Destroy everything!' demanded Ramiel.

Chapter 20 - Daniel Walks Away From Hope

Daniel was emotionally and physically exhausted after his encounter with Ramiel. He had thought he was strong, but now he realised how weak he really was, or at least thought he was.

'The Shattered Lord is right', he thought, 'I am of no use to anyone.'

With that depressing thought, he trudged his way to the top of a low hill overlooking the battlefield. He stopped on the crest, turned around and looked down on the scene. In the distance he could see the sky glowing with the fires from the Shattered Lord and around the castle he saw many splinter cats.

'It's hopeless', he thought to himself.

His gaze wandered to the army of the Glassmaker. All bright and shining, apart from the rescued families. His family. His heart jumped within him as he thought of them.

'It's safer if I leave them'.

The Glassmaker's army looked so fearless, organised and confident, so loyal! It angered him.

'I don't know what to think anymore!' he shouted into the cold air. 'Are you good? Are you for us or are you deceiving us? Maybe I should go and warn all of those poor soldiers that you are not who they think you are'

He hung his head.

'Or maybe you are and I am the one who has been deceived', he said gently. 'Have I got it all wrong?'

Daniel's thoughts went to the day he and Ruth had gone through the furnace. How they had been healed. How they had trusted the Glassmaker and how they had laughed together. The memories were good and he started to feel that maybe he had been deceived all along.

At that moment a dark cloud appeared over him, although he didn't see it. It covered his head and Ramiel spoke to him, although Daniel didn't realise it was Ramiel.

'He let Jonah die. He will let you die. He will let your family die. He is a deceiver and He is not good', whispered Ramiel.

'They are better off without me. I am right about the Glassmaker. There is something suspicious about him!'

When Ramiel saw that his work was done, the dark cloud disappeared.

Daniel looked at the scene for another moment, turned around and walked away from the Glassmaker and his army.

Chapter 21 - Daniel's Encounter

Daniel's despondency deepened the further he walked away from the Glassmaker. His sense of loss grew as he took each step and that sense of loss fortified the doubt and anger that he harboured. Occasionally the loss led him to a sadness that he was leaving the Glassmaker, but he quickly pushed that aside.

The ground he walked on was rocky and he stumbled and fell. Each time he tripped over a rock he shouted out in anger.

After walking for what seemed like hours, he sat down wearily and realised that he had brought nothing to eat or drink.

'Arghh!' he cried out and hit the ground with his hand creating a cloud of dust.

He spluttered as the dust rose up and filled his mouth, making him even more thirsty. He lifted his dust covered face to the sky and yelled once more. He was doing a lot of that lately, yelling. As he did so, little channels of tears ran down his dusty face.

A noise disturbed his tantrum and he looked around fearfully. All he could see was a flock of silver birds standing on a rock nearby.

'Come to gloat, have you?' he said, 'I don't blame you.'

Suddenly, the birds took flight towards him and he was under the impression, mistakenly, that they were going to attack him.

'Shoo', he screeched as he waved his hands over his head trying to beat them away, 'leave me alone.'

However, they weren't attacking him. As suddenly as they had appeared, they disappeared and Daniel was alone again in the barren stillness. He looked around to make sure they had gone, brushing the dust from himself and muttering about how much worse could it get, when he noticed a pile of food in front of him.

'Where on earth did that come from?' he thought, but he was so hungry, he didn't think too much about it and dived straight in the food. As he ate, he started to become thankful for the food.

'I wonder if the birds brought the food, but why would they do that?' he wondered. Then he remembered some words the Glassmaker had said about not worrying and trusting in him to provide for all of their needs. His heart softened a little. Then the ground shook.

He looked around as the pebbles and stone vibrated. A crack appeared in the ground beside him.

'So you fed me up, just so the ground could swallow me!' he shouted, his gratitude quickly disappearing.

He stood up and edged away from the split in the ground, but with his eyes firmly fixed on it. It grew and then the ground gave way and a sink-hole appeared. The ground stopped trembling and all was still once again. Daniel remained fixated by the new hole, wondering what it could mean. However, the stillness didn't last long as a faint gurgling came from deep within the ground. The gurgling increased in volume and the dust in the hole darkened as water miraculously appeared, creating a spring of water.

Daniel dived eagerly to the ground and drank deeply,

quenching his thirst. Breathless from drinking quickly, he burst into tears as he knelt.

'Is this you?' he questioned looking around into the emptiness, 'Glassmaker, is this all your doing?'

He put his hands to his face and let his forehead touch the ground. He felt a weight pressing down on him. Not a sound could be heard, for the quietness deepened. Daniel was aware of a presence beside him. For a moment, he was too afraid to look up. Then he heard his name spoken, 'Daniel.'

Daniel broke down, weeping uncontrollably as he recognised the voice. He gradually looked up and there, glowing and shining brighter than he thought possible, was the Glassmaker.

Chapter 22 - Daniel Is Restored

Daniel was speechless and humbled by the presence of the Glassmaker.

'I turned my back on you', he said.

'I never turned my back on you, replied the Glassmaker, 'I always have and always will love you. All things will be well.'

Daniel wept until the ground in front of him was darkened by his tears. The Glassmaker knelt down and lifted Daniel's head.

'It is going to be okay', He said gently, 'What Ramiel meant for harm, I will turn into good.'

'How is that possible?' asked Daniel, sniveling through the tears.

'It's possible because I make it possible. I know it looks like an evenly-balanced battle at the moment, but it is not. We already have overwhelming victory. The way I do things is not like the way glass people do things. The way I think is not like the way you think', the Glassmaker replied.

'I don't understand', said Daniel.

'You don't have to. You need faith', said the Glassmaker.

'Faith for what?' Daniel asked.

'Faith to follow the path I will show you', answered the Glassmaker.

Daniel sighed and sat back on the ground. He was covered in dust and his face was filthy with tear-stained rivulets running down it. He shook his head.

'Why on earth would you help me or let me be part of your plan? I betrayed you! I am weak!' he said.

'I love weak people', said the Glassmaker, 'I love seeing them transformed into courageous followers.'

The Glassmaker looked at the sky.

'The sun is going down. It will be dark soon and will get cold. Look up the mountain.'

The Glassmaker was pointing and Daniel followed the direction of his finger.

'Do you see the cave halfway up?'

'Yes', answered Daniel.

'Go to that cave and you will be shown the path', said the Glassmaker, and with those words He disappeared and Daniel was alone again.

Daniel pondered on what had just happened. Again, he had been changed by a simple encounter with the Glassmaker. He felt clean on the inside, even though he was covered in dust on the outside. He felt loved again and accepted. He would not let this encounter fade, but let the effects of it grow in him. He would not turn his back on the Glassmaker again. One of the birds that had brought him food had come back and was perched on a rock. Daniel smiled.

'Thanks for bringing me food. Now, I have a mountain to climb.'

Chapter 23 - Daniel Enters The Cave

The mountains hadn't seemed quite so far away when Daniel had looked at them with the Glassmaker. By the time he reached the foothills it was very dark and cold. He kept stumbling over rocks he couldn't see and his anger was rising again.

'Calm down!' he said to himself, choosing a different response to the difficulties he was now facing.

He stopped and looked around, but he could see nothing. He looked up in the direction of the shadowed mountain and he saw a light emanating from what must be the cave. It was the only light around. He took it as his guide and stepped onto the mountain. The climb was difficult and the only way he could make sense of where he was going was by keeping his focus on the light. In that way he wouldn't drift off in the wrong direction.

Eventually he made it to the outside of the cave. The light was much stronger and he had to shield his eyes from the brightness.

'What now?' he thought to himself.

He looked back down the way he had come up and the darkness seemed so much darker after looking into the light. He turned back to the cave and was once again blinded, but as he shielded his eyes and continued to try and look into the cave, he thought he saw some movement from inside. Some of the light was shimmering and was not quite as bright as the light in the cave. And it was moving. Or at least it seemed to be moving, as it was getting closer and larger. Daniel took a step back, frightened by the movement. He waited, ready to run if necessary.

'Daniel', whispered a voice from the cave. 'Don't be afraid. I am here to help you.'

Daniel didn't say anything.

'Daniel', whispered the voice again, the movement increasing.

'Who are you? What are you?' said Daniel, finally finding the courage to speak.

The figure emerged from the cave. It was the hermit of the forest. Daniel ran up to him, relieved it wasn't someone from the Shattered Lord, but a friend. They embraced.

'I am so thankful to see you. I ran away from the Glassmaker because I listened to the voice of Ramiel and then I met the Glassmaker on the road, and can you believe it, He provided for me and forgave me. And He told me to come to this cave, and now you're here!'

Daniel had spoken so fast he was breathless.

'Yes, I am here', said the hermit, 'and I am so glad to see you.'

'You look younger', Daniel said.

The hermit smiled, 'The Glassmaker is good - always.'

Daniel nodded, 'I know that now for sure. Why are you here?'

'To show you the next step. Follow me.'

Daniel hesitated for a moment and then followed the hermit into the cave.

Caves are normally dark places, but this cave was full of light. The light was warm and inviting, but it was hard to follow the hermit due to the brightness.

'Where are we going?' he asked.

'You'll see ', was the only reply he got.

After a time, the light seemed to be coming to an end and they stepped out of the cave into an enormous chasm in the centre of the mountain. The chasm opened out onto the sky and he could see the stars high above. Daniel looked up, amazed at how big the chasm was. There was nothing there except a tree in the middle. The most beautiful and fragrant tree he had ever encountered.

'I must go now, 'said the hermit.

'What! Why?' stuttered Daniel, 'What is that tree?'

'I have played my role and that tree is the second tree, the fruit of which will bring healing and restoration.'

Chapter 24 - Daniel Speaks To The Second Tree

'Wait', said Daniel, but the hermit was gone. He looked around to see if the hermit was simply hiding, but he soon realised that he was completely alone. He was scared. Trees are not normally scary things, but the last time he had encountered a tree, the first tree, Daniel and Ruth and the others had been put through different tests and temptations. The first tree had very nearly imprisoned them. Understandably, Daniel was nervous of this second tree, no matter what the hermit had said.

He looked back at the cave and started to walk back into it, to try and get away from the tree.

'Come to me, and don't be afraid.'

Daniel stopped walking, his heart beating fast.

'Who said that?' he said nervously.

'I did', came the reply.

Daniel turned around expecting to see somebody, but no-one was there.

'Why are you hiding from me?'

'I am not hiding from you. I am right in front of you', answered the voice.

The tree swayed even though the air was still and Daniel realised that the tree was the one talking.

'No!' said Daniel curtly and turning around quickly, he

headed towards the cave. He remembered the pain from his last encounter with a tree.

'Wait', said the second tree, 'I am not like the first tree. I am different. I have come to restore, not to destroy, to set free, not to imprison.'

There was a gentleness and a warmth in the tree's voice that drained the fear from Daniel. He turned to face the tree. It looked very different from the first tree. That tree had been thorny, craggy and grey, whereas the second tree was smooth, colourful and, well, beautiful. It emanated a glow and Daniel could now feel the thrumming of its life, like a pulse.

'Come closer', it said, 'and hear what I have to say.'

Daniel obeyed and sat down in front of the tree. He noticed that gorgeous fruits hung from its branches and the sight of them made him want to take one and eat. He, unknowingly, stood up and was about to pick one of the fruits, when the tree spoke.

'Not yet. Let me talk first.'

Daniel shook his head and came to his senses.

'I am so sorry', he said, 'I didn't realise what I was doing. It was as though the fruit was calling me to eat it.'

'The fruit is important and you will take it soon, but first I must speak', said the tree.

The tree continued to speak as Daniel sat in front of it, listening.

'The first tree was first, but it was not before me.'

'What?' said a confused Daniel, 'What on earth does that mean?'

'Don't worry about understanding, it takes time', said the tree, 'as I was saying, the first tree was first. The Glassmaker created it to give fruit and shelter and life to the emerging glass kingdom. However, over time the tree saw that what it had was good and wanted to keep it for itself. At that time, Ramiel became friends with the tree, and together they refused to give the things the tree was supposed to give and the tree hardened and Ramiel become more broken. The tree and Ramiel both wanted to be more than they were and they have been trying to take for themselves ever since.'

'I've experienced that!' said Daniel, 'but what about you, why are you here?'

'It's hard to explain. I came from the heart of the Glassmaker. I was not created, but birthed from him. I am part of the Glassmaker and you must now pick my fruit and then I will die.'

Chapter 25 - Daniel Takes The Fruit

Daniel jumped up, confused and horrified at what the second tree had just said.

'What do you mean?' he said, his words stumbling over each other, 'You die because I pick the fruit that you have just told me not to touch. Why would I do that? '

The tree swayed gently, and what sounded like singing arose as it swayed.

'The ways of the Glassmaker are not our ways. They are much higher and better. The seed my fruit contains brings hope. You must take the fruit to the Glassmaker. This is your path, your calling. It's the safest path for you.'

'But why must you die? Why do I need to give the fruit to the Glassmaker?' Daniel asked, with more confusion and more questions arising with each of his thoughts.

'You would not understand even if I told you. You only see in shadows. What will happen will look like defeat. But it is not defeat. It is victory!' replied the tree.

As Daniel was about to respond, he heard rocks falling in the distance.

'What was that? Who's there?' he shouted.

Nothing responded.

'If you don't take the fruit to the Glassmaker, you will not understand', continued the tree, unfazed by the falling rocks.

'People think you understand by your thoughts, but you really understand by your actions. Friendship leads to trusting and trusting leads to action and obedience. Daniel, you let go of your anchor, you chose to walk by doubt. Now is the time to choose, once again, to walk by faith. The Glassmaker is good, you are loved and He is powerful and strong.'

The tree finished speaking and started to sway again as the sound of music filled the air. Daniel heard more rocks falling and he knew that someone, or something, was there.

'Quick', he said to the tree, 'We must do something. There is something else here.'

The tree stopped swaying.

'Take one of my fruits', it said, lowering one of its branches so that Daniel could reach it. He hesitated, knowing that the tree would die.

'Don't hesitate, Daniel. I willingly do this. Take my fruit and give it to the Glassmaker.'

Daniel reached up and held the fruit in his hands. He looked once more at the tree, sadness in his heart, and plucked the fruit from the branch. The tree shuddered and slowly the tree's light started to fade, as the light dims during a sunset.

Daniel was left in the fading light, when he heard the screeching of splinter cats.

Chapter 26 - Daniel And The Splinter Cats

The screeching unnerved Daniel.

'That was more than one splinter cat', he thought, 'how can I survive this? '

At that point he sensed that the dimming tree was trying to speak to him in his thoughts. Initially, he resisted, unsure what was happening and scarred by what happened when Ramiel entered his thoughts. The situation was dire, so he relented, allowing the tree access to his thoughts.

'You cannot defeat all of these splinter cats. You need to see them and name them to have any chance of surviving.'

'What do you mean 'name them'?' asked Daniel, searching the sky for attacking splinter cats.

'Splinter cats are glass people who have completely forgotten who they are. They have forgotten what it is to have a name and be known. As they attack, look at them. Look at their eyes, and ask the Glassmaker to give you their original names', said the tree.

It sounded very strange to Daniel, but he had no other options and had to trust in the words of the second tree.

'I will help until I am unable', said the tree.

Then suddenly, 'Look up!'

Daniel looked up and an enormous splinter cat was diving straight at him. He had no time to evade the cat, far less to think of naming it, whatever good that might do. The splinter cat hit him with its talons and flew upwards. Another came and then another. Daniel was knocked to the ground and pummeled. He curled his body around the fruit to protect it.

'You are not getting this', he said to the cats although they weren't listening. There was a brief lull in the attack and Daniel glanced upwards. He saw another cat heading towards him to attack. This was his chance.

'Glassmaker, please help me know the name of this cat', he prayed. He looked straight at the oncoming attacker, his heart pounding. It was getting closer and closer. Suddenly a name came to him.

'Florence', he shouted. 'You are called Florence.'

At the sound of the name the splinter cat faltered as though its wings were not working properly, and it started to change shape. Now it was no longer flying, but tumbling in the sky and it was getting smaller. It was still coming towards him, but he was not scared anymore. The former splinter cat fell from the sky and landed in front of him. It was no longer a splinter cat, but a glass woman. She looked at Daniel through dying eyes, a smile on her face.

She whispered, 'Thank you for calling my name. Thank you for reminding me of who I am.'

With those moving words, she closed her eyes and died. Daniel only had a moment to look at her as more and more splinter cats were coming towards him and he started to call the names the Glassmaker gave to him. Splinter cats morphed and fell to the ground as glass people. Glass people set free. They all died, thankful for their freedom. However, there were so many to name and some of the cats managed to strike Daniel and he soon fell back on the ground being beaten by them. As he fell, he looked at all of the glass people lying on the ground and such a love and compassion arose within him for them, and for the splinter cats, that he felt no anger towards the cats hitting him, but sorrow at what they were enduring. The attack intensified. Daniel could only occasionally call out a name and another glass person would fall to the ground, freed from their captivity, but eventually it was all too much and he passed out, vaguely aware of a thundering noise and his name being called out.

Chapter 27 - Lava

The closer that Ruth, Jade, Nathaniel and Noah got to the cave in the mountain, the more they realised that this was no ordinary cave.

'Shouldn't there be darkness in a cave, not light?' asked Jade.

They could hear noises in the sky and from the mountain and then they felt the ground shaking.

"Splinter cats!" shouted Noah. "take cover."

They all ran quickly to the cave over the shuddering ground. They reached the cave, breathless and hesitant to enter, but the threat of attack compelled them to go in.

They looked at the sky once more and then ran into the shining cave.

'Did anyone else notice that the cats didn't seem to want to attack us?' said Ruth.

'I did', answered Jade.

They had all noticed that, but no-one had an answer as to why.

Once in the cave they had to shield their eyes as it was so bright.

'Let's go farther in and find a safe place to camp for the night', said Noah, 'even though it's like daytime in here.'

'I'm not sure how I'm going to sleep in all this light and the ground shaking, but I feel safer here in the light than outside in the darkness', said Jade, and the others agreed.

'The light seems to dim over there', Nathaniel pointed out and they walked towards the spot he had indicated. All of a sudden they found themselves outside the cave in the centre of the mountain watching splinter cats attack a person lying on the ground and many glass people lying all around. There was a tree in the middle and it was causing the shaking of the ground.

Ruth realised who the shining one was lying on the ground.

'Daniel!' she screamed and ran as fast as she could towards him, ignoring the attacking splinter cats. She reached him and knelt down beside him. Nathaniel, Jade and Noah had followed her and stood around them, trying to fend off the attacking splinter cats.

'Daniel', she cried and shook him a little.

Daniel's eyes opened slightly and he smiled.

'What took you so long?'

Ruth smiled back and looked at the fruit and then to the tree.

'This tree is good', he said to Ruth, 'and I need to get its fruit to the Glassmaker.'

'Easier said than done', replied Ruth looking up and seeing many splinter cats preparing to attack. At that point the ground started to heave even more and rocks fell from the surrounding slopes, hitting some of the cats. The tree then began to glow a deep red and started to sink into the ground creating a vast cauldron of spurting fire and lava, which hit more of the cats.

'Run!', came the cry from the tree.

Noah shouted, 'Let's go to the cave. This is our best chance!'

Noah and Ruth picked up Daniel and made towards the

cave, whilst Jade and Nathaniel defended them from attack. They were knocked to the ground, not by splinter cats, but by the ferocity of the shaking ground and they tripped over some of the many glass people who lay lifeless around them. Lava was pouring out of the newly created lava pool and was getting closer to them.

'Quickly!' yelled Jade.

The lava got closer and closer. Just as it was about to reach them they made it to the cave and kept running. A strange thing happened. The lava didn't enter the cave. It stopped as though an invisible wall stood there. The lava piled up until the entrance to the cave was blocked off and they were safe.

They nearly jumped out of themselves when the hermit suddenly appeared and welcomed them.

Chapter 28 - Ramiel And Tabbris

The Shattered Lord had been watching the whole scene unfold. He had seen Daniel abandon the Glassmaker. He had seen the food and water provided. He had seen the encounter with the Glassmaker, but he was unable to hear what was being said. Although he was angry that the Glassmaker had apparently helped Daniel, Ramiel danced around the throne room as he watched the second tree die and sink into the ground.

'At last, that disgusting second tree is now destroyed! What a beautiful thing to happen!' he said with sneering voice. He was moving around the room in an apparent effort to dance, so happy was he, but it was not a beautiful thing to see. It was an ugly and stompy kind of dance that made you want to look away with embarrassment.

'But!' he said suddenly stopping his grotesque dancing. All in the room wondered what he was going to say, knowing that it would not be a pat on the back for all of their work and service.

'But!' he screamed, 'Why are Daniel and all of his sniveling little troop still alive?'

He stamped on the ground as he said these last words and the glass floor started to crack under the pounding. All in the room lowered their eyes, apart from Tabbris, who stood near

Ramiel. A hint of defiance and compassion was creeping into his heart and face, but it was not for Ramiel, but for Daniel. Fortunately, Ramiel did not see it.

'The most infuriating thing is that I can't now access Daniel's mind, and I do so want to cause him pain', said Ramiel.

He looked around the room and started to smile hideously. He lifted his head and some in the room started to cry out in pain. The louder they cried out in pain the more pain Ramiel inflicted. Numerous cracks appeared in their disfigured bodies and Ramiel started to laugh. Tabbris watched in horror as Ramiel caused suffering. Tabbris had followed Ramiel during the great war with the Glassmaker and he had initially thought the Glassmaker had been the one to inflict suffering. Over time Tabbris had realised that the Glassmaker was good and that Ramiel was the one filled with evil. He had made a mistake turning his back on the Glassmaker. He had hidden this regret for so long. Now seeing Ramiel hurt his own followers, tipped Tabbris over the edge.

'Stop it! That is enough!' he shouted.

Ramiel stopped walking around and those he had been hurting fell to the ground as the pain stopped. He turned to face Tabbris.

'What did you say? No, it's okay, I know what you said. I heard you Tabbris. You are a traitor, disloyal to the Glassmaker and now disloyal to me. You are a person who belongs to no-one. You are now nameless, a nobody!'

With each word spoken by Ramiel pain spread through Tabbris, until he was kneeling on the floor. He looked up at Ramiel.

'I was disloyal to the Glassmaker and I so regret that. He loves me!' he gasped through the pain, 'but I have no loyalty to you. I would go back to the Glassmaker without hesitation if I could.'

Those last words inflamed Ramiel. His anger boiled over and Tabbris exploded into a thousand pieces. All of those in the room gasped and took steps away from Ramiel. Ramiel remained still looking at where Tabbris had been. He lifted his eyes and looked at all in the room with more hatred than they had ever seen. The four fires raged all the more at the intensity of his hatred and continued their destructive paths across the glass kingdom. People were still fleeing from their homes to escape the devastation taking over their world. Not everyone escaped. However, with the Glassmaker there is always hope.

Chapter 29 - Leaving The Cave

The hermit had startled them even though his voice was gentle. It was just unexpected. Ruth and Noah set Daniel down on the ground.

'I am fine', he said bravely, 'I just need to rest for a moment.'

He was still clutching the fruit from the tree as he lay on the ground. The hermit walked over to him and knelt down. He placed his hand on the fruit and smiled.

'The seed with this fruit will restore the things that need to be restored', he said, 'You must keep it safe and deliver it to the Glassmaker.'

'What do you mean that the seed of this fruit is special?' asked Ruth.

'It's more than special. The second tree and the Glassmaker are one. The tree has sacrificed itself to save the kingdom.'

'How can this be?' asked Nathaniel.

The hermit didn't say anything for a while. He just kept staring at the fruit. Eventually he replied.

'Not everything will be explained. You simply must have faith in the Glassmaker.'

They all looked at one another. Daniel gingerly sat up and spoke.

'What do we do next?'

'You must walk out of the front of the cave', replied the hermit.

'That's madness!' said Jade. 'The splinter cats will have simply flown over the mountain and will attack us as soon as we leave the cave. We don't stand a chance. We need a better plan.'

Noah put his hand up and she stopped speaking. It wasn't until there was silence she realised that she had been speaking with a raised voice.

'Sorry', she said.

The gentle hermit once again smiled and put his hand on her shoulder.

'Your passion is such an inspiration to those around you on the battlefield, but let your faith increase and walk out of the cave. All things will be well.'

He spoke softly, but with authority and Jade nodded, drew out her sword and started walking out of the cave.

'Wait', called Ruth, 'let's go together.'

They helped Daniel to his feet and held hands. Jade put her sword away.

'Swords won't defend us this time', said Ruth. 'There are simply too many splinter cats. Better if we are united, together.'

They all walked out of the cave, hearts beating, not knowing what was going to happen, but obedient. They stepped out of the cave, expecting a barrage of splinter cats. Instead, they stood on the battlefield, facing the Shattered Lord's castle, and standing next to the Glassmaker. He looked at them.

'Welcome back!'

Chapter 30 - The Challenge

They were all so relieved at being with the Glassmaker that they burst out laughing. It was infectious and the soldiers, who had been just as startled when they appeared out of nowhere, burst out laughing with them.

'You gave us quite a shock', said one of the soldiers, 'One minute there was nothing and next minute you all appear out of thin air.'

'We wondered where you had all gone', said another. 'We are glad you're back.'

The Glassmaker turned his attention back to the Shattered Lord, who was shouting from his castle. It was obvious that he was getting angrier.

'Do you have the fruit, Daniel?' asked the Glassmaker.

Daniel lifted up the fruit and handed it to the Glassmaker, who took it and put it in a large pocket inside his cloak.

'Thank you for rescuing me and not rejecting me', said Daniel. 'If it wasn't for your love, I don't know what would have happened to me.'

Daniel's voice choked on the emotions that started to rise to the surface. Tears began to well up.

'You are worth rescuing.' He replied. 'All of you are. I do not want to lose one person.'

As He said these last words, He looked back at Ramiel,

who was still ranting from the ramparts of his castle.

'You have all been deceived', he yelled, 'the Glassmaker is not who you think He is. He is not good!'

As Ramiel said this, angry murmurs started to rise among the Glassmaker's soldiers.

Ramiel continued, 'He does not love you. He only has his own interests at heart. As soon as He gets what He wants, He will abandon you, just as He abandoned me!'

The Glassmaker's soldiers were now starting to shout back at Ramiel.

Despite the noise from the shining soldiers Ramiel continued shouting, 'He is not faithful and He will let you down and disfigure you! Trust me instead.'

The whole of the shining army was roaring and ready to attack as soon as the word was given. Eventually the roaring subsided and into the growing stillness Ramiel issued a challenge to the Glassmaker.

'You know that you will be okay when the fires arrive here. But your people will be melted. Give yourself up! If you do then I promise that all of your people will be treated fairly and I will stop the fires coming from the four corners.'

Where there had been angry roaring from the shining army, it now turned to laughter at the suggestion that the Glassmaker turn himself in and surrender. The laughter stopped as soon as they all watched the Glassmaker walk towards Ramiel's castle.

Chapter 31 - It Looks Like Defeat

The soldiers thought that with the Glassmaker moving towards the castle the attack was imminent, so they followed him. The Glassmaker stopped and turned around.

'Stop', he said, 'and put away your swords. This will not end by fighting, but by surrender and sacrifice. This may look like defeat, but it is victory.'

'What?!'

'No!'

'What's He doing?!'

The Glassmaker looked around and then his eyes rested on Daniel and Ruth. He smiled at them. As Daniel looked, he remembered his encounter with the Glassmaker when doubt had twisted his thoughts.

'What was it He said?' Daniel thought. He looked away for a moment trying to recollect the words that had been spoken to him. He looked back at the Glassmaker.

'The way I do things is not like the way glass people do things and the way I think is not the way glass people think', He said loudly.

Ruth looked at Daniel and then at the Glassmaker, trying to fathom what was going on.

'Yes, that's right', said the Glassmaker. He knelt down beside Daniel and Ruth and put his hands on their shoulders.

'Continue to have faith in me. Now, more than ever. Guide the glass people. They will not understand what I am about to do', He said to them both.

The Glassmaker stood up, turned towards the castle and made his way to the entrance. Again, the soldiers started to follow, but Ruth and Daniel stood in their way.

'What are you doing?' asked one of the troop leaders, 'We must follow our lord!'

'Out of the way! We are here to fight.' said a very large soldier.

Daniel and Ruth held hands and stood firm.

'No', said Ruth, 'the Glassmaker will walk this path alone. You will not understand it until later. I don't really understand, but we must have faith that all things will be well.'

Frustration and discontent were growing in the front line of the troops and they tried to push past Ruth and Daniel, but Daniel put his hand up.

'You shall not go this way! We need to trust and obey!'

As the Glassmaker neared the castle entrance, the restlessness increased. They could see the Shattered Lord dancing in his throne room above and that stirred up within them a ferocious desire to fight.

'Out of our way now!' yelled another shining soldier.

'No!' came a voice, and Nathaniel, Noah and Jade came to stand side by side with their friends. 'We will have faith! Together.'

As they stood there, the Glassmaker reached the entrance of the castle. The gates opened and He walked inside.

Chapter 32 - The Glassmaker In Ramiel's Castle

Ramiel rushed down to the entrance of his castle to greet the Glassmaker. He was almost happy. Almost. He pushed past his grey soldiers and arrived at the gates breathless with exertion and anticipation. He really hadn't thought the Glassmaker would accept his proposal. But here was the mighty Glassmaker voluntarily walking into Ramiel's castle.

'Welcome, welcome! At last you are mine and I am going to get my revenge', said Ramiel. 'Surround him and chain him!'

Immediately the Glassmaker was chained and surrounded by hundreds of malevolent soldiers. They were angrily pushing one another out of the way to get closer to the Glassmaker and somehow cause him pain or humiliate him. The Glassmaker gently spoke out the names of the soldiers who spat at him or struck him.

'Gabriel, Michael, Luke, Martha…' He said.

As the names were called out the distorted soldiers briefly remembered who they once had been and they pulled away in pain. The Glassmaker did not want to cause any pain. He wanted them to remember who they were, but the process of remembering can sometimes be painful.

'Gag him!' said Ramiel aggressively, as he saw what the Glassmaker was doing. 'Don't let him speak. How the mighty have fallen. Look at you. How I have waited for this moment. Do you realise how much pain and suffering you have caused! It was not my fault, but yours!'

Ramiel was getting more and more animated as he spoke.

'And do you really think that I am going to treat your people well after what you have done to me? I am going to destroy you and then I am going to destroy those who will not follow me! No mercy! The fires will not be stopped. In fact, I am going to make them burn all the hotter.'

He stopped, breathing heavily from his outburst. The Glassmaker did not struggle.

'I am going to melt you down. Take him to the furnace!' said Ramiel and the horde of soldiers poked and prodded the Glassmaker with their swords and forced him to move towards the furnace room.

The room was suffocating with the heat that the furnace was making. Ramiel was overcome with excitement. He took a sword from one of the soldiers and started to hit the Glassmaker repeatedly, forcing him nearer and nearer to the steps of the furnace, until the Glassmaker had nowhere else to go, but into the furnace.

Chapter 33 - Not Doing The Sensible Thing

The Glassmaker's army could see what was happening through the cracked glass walls of the castle. They made ready to attack. Nothing would stop them now. Daniel and Ruth tried, but they were unable and the army moved as one to storm the castle gates. However, there was no way through the barrier that sparked and crackled. They were helpless as they watched the Glassmaker step into the furnace.

He still wore the blindfold as He walked deeper into the furnace, pain etched on his face as the furnace started to melt him. The liquid in the furnace was bubbling furiously, as though excited by who was walking into it.

Ramiel was giddy with excitement as he watched the Glassmaker descend into the fiery pit. He had waited so long to see this and he had never been certain that it would ever happen. Now he was watching the Glassmaker melt.

The Glassmaker continued to go down into the pit. He put his hand into the pocket that contained the fruit that Daniel had had brought back.

'All will be well', He said to himself.

As He uttered these words, He felt his legs buckle under him and with nothing to give him support, He slid into the furnace and could be seen no more. There was complete silence inside and outside the castle. Silence inside, because they were unsure whether they had won or not. Outside, because it looked like they had been defeated. They had just witnessed the impossible. The defeat of the Glassmaker. They hung their heads and wept.

Ramiel stood waiting, looking into the furnace to make sure that the Glassmaker really had been defeated. When he was sure, he let out a scream that released all of the pain that he had felt for so long. The pain that he had created, even though he thought the Glassmaker had created it.

'Destroy them all!' he cried out, pointing at the Glassmaker's army. Splinter cats and grey soldiers poured out of the castle onto a disbelieving army. Empowered by the defeat of the Glassmaker they struck with such force that many of the shining soldiers were struck down before they had a chance to realise what was happening. The fires in the distance burned with greater intensity as the fury of Ramiel was released. Daniel and Ruth defended themselves from the onslaught, but they had nowhere to go, or purpose to fight for. They looked around and saw the chaos that was being created by the Shattered Lord's army. They looked at each other and knew what they were each thinking. It seemed so long ago that they had been playing tricks on Constable Bunce in the little village of Knock. They had been through so much. They had been changed beyond recognition. In that moment of apparent defeat, they knew that to try and fight with swords would be pointless. The enemy was too strong and too numerous. The sensible thing was to fight for their lives. The wise thing to do was surrender. Not surrender to the enemy, but to the purposes of the Glassmaker, whatever they might be. They had to continue to trust. They threw down their swords and knelt down in the middle of the battlefield. At first, they were the only ones, but soon others joined them and the Glassmaker's army knelt in surrender to their King and called upon his name. They sang out in praise of him. It didn't seem logical, but it was the right thing to do.

Everything seemed to move in slow motion around them. It seemed like defeat, but they prayed that it was not. Faith and worship were their weapons, not swords.

The ground gently shook, almost imperceptible at first, but soon it grew in intensity. The attacking enemy were now unsteady on their feet as the quaking grew in intensity. The walls of the castle started to shake. Ramiel looked around, unclear as to what was happening. Pieces of roof started to fall down around him. It was then he heard the bubbling of the furnace. It spluttered as though it was trying to get rid of something. Slowly and steadily, the Glassmaker walked up the steps on the opposite side of the furnace. Walls collapsed, soldiers fell down with no life in them, as the Glassmaker walked.

Ramiel stared in disbelief at the Glassmaker. The furnace was not yet finished. It churned and bubbled, as a tree started to grow out of it. It grew fast and consumed the furnace, until the furnace was no more and the second tree stood tall in Ramiel's castle. The Glassmaker walked towards Ramiel, who shrank back into the shadows, his face marked with pain and anger.

'It cannot be! How can you be alive!' he screamed. He cracked more as the Glassmaker approached. Through the cracks, the true Ramiel could be seen, the Ramiel the Glassmaker had originally created. He looked longingly at the Glassmaker, bowed his head and Ramiel shattered into thousands of pieces.

Chapter 34 - New Things

A wind blew through the battlefield as soon as Ramiel had shattered, disintegrating the grey soldiers into dust. The splinter cats fell from the sky and disappeared as they fell. The four fires disappeared. Only the Glassmaker's army was left standing on the battlefield. Ramiel's castle crumbled, leaving only the Glassmaker standing in front of the new second tree.

The second tree had similarities to the tree Daniel had encountered in the mountain, but this one was more glorious, more beautiful. The colours were more vibrant and the fruits looked far more delicious. The shining ones, gathered around the Glassmaker and knelt in wonder. The families who had been imprisoned were standing at the back, unsure as to what to do. The Glassmaker looked on them with love and beckoned them to come to him. Hesitant at first, they slowly made their way forward and stood before him. They looked so pale and drab next to the Glassmaker. Everyone did. He picked a fruit from the tree and held it out to Daniel's father.

'Eat', the Glassmaker said to him.

Peter, Daniel's father, took the fruit and opened it up. Inside there were many seeds, like a pomegranate. He took a bite. After a moment he started to glow and change. His family stood back, unsure what was happening. He grew brighter and brighter. He increased in height and he laughed. He had been transformed into a shining one! He quickly gave the fruit to his family and soon all who had been imprisoned were shining ones. There was a roar from all of the other shining ones and a party started. Dancing and laughter filled the place, where fighting and pain had existed. The tree started to thrum with life and started to sway in joy. The trunk of the tree started to glow even brighter. Daniel looked at the Glassmaker trying to work out what was happening.

'Go and see', the Glassmaker said to him.

Daniel, Ruth, Noah, Jade and Nathaniel made their way to the tree. They had to shield their eyes from the light. They kept looking at it as best they could and they began to see movement from within. The movement shimmered and grew. Within a few moments, Ranger and Firestone stood before them and Noah, Nathaniel and Jade ran to them, almost knocking them over in their joy. Many more people started to walk out of the tree. Tabbris walked out, completely overwhelmed by the love of the Glassmaker. Daniel and Ruth continued to look at another shimmering shape walking towards them. It was Jonah.

The Glassmaker laughed and declared, 'I am making all things new. All will be well!'

THE END

Printed in Great Britain
by Amazon

84873589R00153